ISBN-10: 1543188362
ISBN-13: 978-154318863

Ok.

This is a work of fiction and any resemblances to persons alive or dead is entirely coincidental and unintentional. This is also a work of entertainment and not to be used in any conversation that includes the phrase "wake up, Sheeple!" Nor should this work be interpreted as encouragement to any violent anti-government activity. If you find that your mind has been filled with dangerous and violent thoughts triggered by any of the following chapters, please seek professional counseling.

Now, if you find yourself existentially frustrated with the state of modern politics at any given point while reading this book then, well, welcome to the club.

Why don't you go write a book about it.

To America,

This book
Is an excorcism

THE LEAST OF 99 EVILS

Pierre Manchot

The End of Benny Greere

Benny Greere has forgotten it is election day. He catches
his breath and steals a look around the bend to see if
they are still after him: the Servicemen. Benny owns a
gun, but he has left it at home, upstairs in a shoebox in a
drawer, never thinking he would ever actually need it.
The Servicemen hadn't given him the time to grab it.
They're pushy like that. He curses at himself, thinking
how he could have easily escaped from the second story
window of his house and shimmied down a nearby tree,
gun tucked in his jeans. Hindsight and all that. He takes
another peek around the corner and sees the black sedan
creep along the street, no doubt looking for him.

Benny rubs his eyes and then he gets running again.
People stare at him with a look of pity. He's sure that
they *know*, oblivious McDonald's-breakfast-eating cretins
though they may be. Benny checks himself in a

storefront window— his shirt is soaked in sweat and his eyes are wild, the size of golf-balls. He looks at his naked feet and winces as they strike the pavement. The Servicemen hadn't given him the time to grab his shoes, either.

Around another corner and he chances a break to catch his breath. Behind him he hears the car gunning, and the sedan slides into his view. Benny breaks for the nearest open building— a parking garage. He runs to the elevator and hits the up button and hides himself in the adjacent stairwell. He hears a car door slam and rubber soles against concrete. The sound echoes as it narrows in on him *à la* reverse echolocation. The elevator arrives and he throws himself inside, hitting the number 7, too clever to go straight to the top.

Benny looks through the glass of the elevator below and sees a traffic incident. A red jeep had apparently enjambed itself between two black sedans. He sees two bodies in the street. Benny doesn't know what that means and he tells himself that it isn't related to his current predicament. He attempts to regain his breath, savoring the temporary sanctuary of the elevator. When it reaches the sixth floor, Benny flattens himself against the wall. When the doors open on seventh, with a pleasant ding, he peers around before taking flight across the lot. He hears the echoes of shoes and slamming doors below him — the Servicemen are gaining.

Benny bounds to the stairwell on the opposite side of the parking structure and hears the clatter of

Servicemen climbing the stairs. He doubles back to the nearest truck and flattens himself against the bed, trying not to breath at all. He closes his eyes.

I imagine it is not without some sweet relief when they find him. Terror, yes, I remember the terror myself, but the relief that he doesn't have to run any more, that a decision has been made, well, I remember that too. The sweet oblivion of fate. The Servicemen yank him from the bed by his ankles and are careful to not let his head hit the pavement. One checks him for weapons while the other holds his arms behind his back. Benny weeps but keeps a stiff upper lip. The Servicemen are used to this. They expect it.

The man who just frisked Benny nods to the man who is holding him.

The Holder releases Benny and brings a nine millimeter pistol to the nape of his neck. The Frisker takes the New Testament out of his pocket and takes Benny's hand and lays it flat on the abridged Bible.

The Frisker asks, "Do you swear to uphold the constitution, Benny James Greere?"

Benny sobs and says that he does.

"Congratulations," says the Frisker. "You are now the President of the New States of America."

And Benny sobs. He sobs as they drag him back into the elevator, that previous sanctuary, and Benny sobs as he's passed through the gathering crowd and into a car. He sobs as the Holder reaches for his gun and is struck with a bullet, collapsing dead on the pavement. Benny sobs as the car peels out with the door still open in view of a bewildered audience of fear and excitement. A few onlookers bounce off the hood of the car as it tears through the streets. The Frisker reaches over Benny to close the car door, but not before punching a guy in the jaw.

Benny sobs as the car hums along, now safe from danger. The city is fading outside the car window, turning to farmland. The Frisker hums an almost familiar tune.

He says, the Frisker, "You know, no one wants to become President. For what it's worth, I don't envy you."

Benny, he's thinking of his kids and his wife. He tries not to sob anymore.

He sniffs and says, "I'm glad it's not personal."

This amuses the Frisker.

"Yeah," he says. "Nothing is." The Frisker looks out the window almost wistfully.

The Frisker recovers from his thoughts and returns to the present. He slaps Benny on the knee.

"It ain't so bad, man. I've seen a few Presidents in my time, and I think you got what it takes."

Benny looks at him incredulously but doesn't say anything. The Frisker takes notice and doesn't add anything further. The car hums along and so does the Frisker.

The scenery outside is completely rural now, plots of soy and wheat with gridded tree lines to help irrigate rainfall. Benny thinks of his kids, Tyson and Greg, two little mischief makers who'd be fatherless for a year. He thinks of his wife, imagining her reading the news the next day that he had been elected and maybe she wouldn't hate him for disappearing like this. He hates it though. He hates the Frisker. He hates the crowd that watched his abduction without protest. Benny hates everything.

"Oh shit," says the Frisker, unholstering his gun. The car brakes to a halt. Benny can see a line of trucks and jeeps blockading the road. To Benny, the Frisker says, "Stay safe. We need you," and hands him his ankle gun, a sweaty .22 caliber pistol. He locks the doors and gets out of the car.

Benny sobs as gunfire rings outside the vehicle. He considers the coward's route, the pistol the Frisker gave him, but he remembers his sons and his wife and he chokes back the impulse. He unlocks the car door and opens it a crack. The Frisker and the driver are firing at a calm, placid rate, taking the time to aim. The attackers, men clad in blue coveralls and bandanas, fire shotguns from the hip. A few of the attackers fall. The driver falls. One more attacker falls before the Frisker follows suit.

Leaving Benny alone with his little .22 pistol. He freezes when the attackers look through the windshield and shudders when the windshield shatters. He regains his senses, taps into something ancient, something primeval and kicks his door open, fires two shots blindly as he ducks into the nearby cornfield. Ears of corn fall to his feet and then he hears the gunfire. He keeps low, ducking and weaving through the stalks. A shape startles behind Benny and he stills it with the .22. He runs and dives, catching on the stalk, and breaking free, crawling, getting back up and firing behind him.

It's dusk now and Benny has reached the end of the cornfield. An acre away, he sees a nice little house sitting on a field of shorn grain. He thinks that'd be a nice place to come back to, if he was given the chance of living again.

His attackers find him on his side in a mud slick. Benny shoots the first to arrive. There's a call backwards to the rest about the live ammo. The second places some buckshot in Benny's legs and approaches to reclaim the fallen gun. He turns Benny on his back.

A figure blocks the sun. A squat, sunburned man with a tobacco stained mustache, wearing a moth-eaten sheriff's uniform stands over Benny.

Heaving, Benny pleads, "I don't want to be President."

Placing a shell into the shotgun, Sheriff chuckles.

He says, "Son, we ain't so keen on the idea neither."

Freedom, Reigned

A lot has happened since you stopped paying attention. For starters, a mob broke past White House security on August 6th, 1974, demanding the head of Richard Milhous Nixon. After some terse negotiations with the secret service, the mob eventually got what they came for. That was the beginning of the end of Washington D.C. After you remove the presidential linchpin, the rest of that dirty old town just fell to ruin. No more Senate. No more House of Representatives. This wasn't the work of a lone gunman, this was democratic rule. And democracy rallied to burn it all to the ground.

Which is what they did. Happily! Congressmen were hunted like elk. Senators like fowl. Some smarties at a university called it anarcho-iconoclasm. I call it whack-a-mole. See, after Nixon got his melon lopped off and D.C. fell apart, that created a power vacuum. And that vacuum would inevitably be filled with a greedy sonuvabitch thirsting for influence— but, every time, roving gangs of Good Ole Americans would run up in their jeeps and put a couple of slugs through any, ahem, *nominees.* 1974 was the year when we didn't have a government.

A frenzied panic took hold of the streets, you could say, and it was a tense time for a lot of people. But for the rest of us, it was a dream come true. People just stopped going to work, now that they didn't have to pay any taxes and by God, once the common folk understood that their landlords were afraid of them, there was no rent to pay. Most of the day was spent farming or spending time with family or friends or devoting the lit hours to a personal craft or art. I became a writer. Or tried to become a writer. What's the difference? In those days I was porch-bound with my typewriter, watching the desert shift its heat all around me.

That golden age didn't last long, for everyone forgot about the one branch of government that hadn't been dissolved: The ARMY. That's right, our boys in green— without executive oversight— had been contemplating whether or not they should instill some martial law and restore order to the United States of America. A lot of us took issue with that and then there was less of us. There was too much instability, too much uncertainty for the common suburbanite, those fools who lived out in little gardens away from their food and means of production. Okay, so the army moved in and told us what was what. But they didn't want to be there any more than we wanted them there. Well, a few generals fancied themselves as keen leaders of a country but they all came down with bad cases of knife-throat while they slept behind well-guarded doors.

So it was a mathematician that came up with a solution. Whether or not it's a *good* solution remains to be seen. The math whiz, his name was Gary Denilles, got some old census records together and wrote a staggeringly simple computer program. It counted the entire American population and ascribed a number to each person and then generated a random number between 1 and the total. So if the population was 215.97 million, which it was, and the computer generated the number 134,097, which it did, then the person assigned to that number, Clyde O'Brien, becomes President for a single year. There was little else to this. If the number called happened to belong to a minor, the vote was thrown out and the program would run again. Thus the Voting Machine was born and a firmer sense of economy was re-established.

Denilles debuted the Voting Machine on Johnny Carson, about the biggest authority Americans kept alive, and talked up the merits of this new system— largely that it was impartial and the service was mandatory. That there would be no benefits, whatsoever, to the lucky number pulled. It's kind of like winning an awful lottery, Denilles admitted, but that would only add a sense of gravitas to the job. A sense of duty, people would say. A burden.

The genius of the plan was how incorruptible it was. Say you get a psychopath in office, a real mean S.O.B. who wants to nuke the Ruskies and invade Mexico, that kind of nonsense. Well, now that he has to organize everything himself (did I mention that almost no aid is given to the President?) he'll quickly grow bored of war mongering and stick his nose back to the grindstone. I'm not being naïve or idealistic here, that actually happened in 1981 when Ralph Cain— yep, the actor— was elected into office by random chance and he attempted a burn on the Soviets. He gave up two days later and went back to lowering taxes for the rich.

That's not to say America still ain't the war machine that it was, it's just that now we're purely a defensive country. We've fought two wars since America's new system. One with North Korea and another with Brazil (right?). And we're still standing, not too much worse for wear.

Except for the entire east and west coasts which were nuked to high hell during Clyde O'Brien's first and only term in office.

America the beautiful, with its beatitudinal red, white and blue, the land that was made for me and you... except it wasn't made for you and me, it wasn't made for anyone, except for maybe the Native tribes that once roamed the land in strong numbers. And it's not red, white and blue, is it? It's a tad gray, isn't it? Because America is factionalized and then factionalized within those factions.

But it sure is beautiful.

After the fall of D.C. some of the more naïve of us figured we'd all fly the banner of a freed nation and get along without the enforcement of the Constitution. It's obvious now that there'd be some resistance to that notion and those that sought to create a new government called themselves the New Americans. The military and former police structures glommed on to this movement thinking it'd be the safest bet to restore order to a wild nation of delinquents. Out of that marriage, and the ensuing boost to recruitment, police and military forces disintegrated and the Servicemen were born. When Denilles offered his solution of the Voting Machine, the Servicemen were quick to enforce his concept.

The other side, those that sought to keep things a bit more *laissez-faire*, called themselves the Old Americans. If you think that's a bit of a lazy handle, well, yeah. The Old Americans weren't keen on organization and that was their point, at least at first: to disrupt any effort to restore America's government. But conflicting opinions will *out* and the anarchistic hippie types of the inner cities that fell in with the Old Americans took issue with the hard-boiled Christian beliefs of the flyover states and vice versa. You've got one side clamoring for communal living and self-sustaining farms and the other side vying for individual freedoms and the right to make a buck for oneself. And hence, the Old Americans cleaved into two separate factions. The religious conservatives called themselves the Good Old Americans and the city liberals called themselves the Frontier.

Then you had the banks, the big businesses and millionaire tycoons, who all purchased private armies to keep their assets safe. I could fill a book, or at least a big pamphlet, with the list of names they came up for their gangs. A few: the Wall, the War Dogs, the Benjamin Brigade, Delta Squad, the Rum Runners, the Skull Mongers... if those sound like intramural hockey team names then wait until you hear about the private armies who contrived their names from sports teams (the Colts, the Knicks, the Bears, the Bullets...) not to mention those who tried to instill a sense of former institutional normalcy by using regional monikers (the Washingtonians, the Michigan Justice Front, New York United).

The religious zealotry of the Good Old Americans created a schism between those who held Christian values above all else and those who felt religious organization was religious persecution in and of itself. Surprise! More factionalization occurred, which is kind of ironic to those who resisted any sort of organization; I suppose it's a bit endearing that people will always need other people whether or not they'll admit to it. Anyway, the Good Old Americans split like buckshot into the Truth Bearers, God's Children, the Angels of Prophecy, the Fishermen, the Mavericks, the John Wayne Brigade (I know!), God's Little Bastards, and the Just, to name a few. These cats like to kill presidential nominees before they have a chance to take office.

A sense of nihilism crept into the Frontier, distinguishing those who sought justice against the betrayal of the Good Old Americans, those who wished to focus on resisting the New Americans and their Servicemen along with some of the more reasonable Good Old American factions, those who simply wanted to burn everything down again and keep it burnt, and those who no longer wished to participate in any kind of violence or conflict whatsoever. As such, the following subgroups were created: the Frontmen, the Thorn of the Rose, Hemlock, Eyes of the Vision, the Haven, the Breaking Point, Enclavius Rex, the Dissent, the Scum, Scorched Heart, and the Harbingers. The more proactive parties liked to kidnap Presidential nominees in the hope that they could influence legislature. That is, when they weren't killing each other.

Then there were those free-lovers who set up more, shall we say, promiscuous parties (the Fornacateurs, Moist Earth, the Vulvateers...), but those guys didn't amount to much in the long game.

Most of America, it should be noted, didn't radicalize. There were people like me who refused to join a faction even though I could have comfortably fit within a few dozen of them. We carried on as usual, working, playing, stressing, eating, loving... I myself was too busy smoking pot and plinking away at the typewriter to care about anything too drastic and that, I felt, was my American duty. Until the other shoe dropped and I got voted into office by the Voting Machine.

Hi, I'm Clyde O'Brien and I'm the first President of the New States of America.

Clyde O'Brien, You Lucky Devil

I'll be brief, because we have to get along to other, more interesting things than my own story. But sure, I'll oblige your curiosity.

When the revolution happened I was playing a gig in Chicago with a blues quartet I'd assembled from some folks I met at a bar in Atlanta. We finished our set and proceeded to get drunk and stoned before falling asleep in someone's van. When the morning came, a new America had already been born. We got breakfast and the waitress asked us if we had read the news, you know, about what happened in D.C. We shook our heads and shuddered through our hangovers and ate our steak and eggs. She said it casually and it didn't quite register. It was only when we drove through St. Louis, when our clarinetist, Abraham, said, "what do you think that means," that it began to sink in.

What did Nixon's execution mean for us? What did it mean that there was no more Congress? I rolled a joint and suffice to say, I didn't answer that question then and I sure as hell haven't since.

My band pulled through our measly tour and returned home to Georgia. I was glad to come home to my wife, Malthilde, my son, Denny, my friends of various names. To my back porch and to my car that didn't drive quite right. Me and Mathilde sipped wine as the sun went down on another humid evening.

And then the riots broke out. A neighbor told me that the Capitol was on fire. When the chaos reached our town, we packed our stuff into my leaky VW and booked it, heading west. The roads were a nightmare, cars backed bumper to bumper and everyone terrified, most of them armed. A few explosions went off on the side of the road and many of us ran to help the injured. Locked in traffic, we shared our water and food with those who suffered from poor foresight (or from just being poor) and pushed those cars who had run out of gas off of the road.

But that was a thing we had never considered—that gas stations would close their doors to the swelling demand. Some of them simply ran out. Others capitalized on the urgency and hiked their rates to a ridiculous heights. We're talking 10 dollars a gallon. We attempted to save as much gasoline as we could, pushing our car ourselves along the bottlenecked roads. We could afford one and a half tankfuls and made it stretch as far as Las Cruces before the VW just up and died. No one had gas to spare. We were out of food, out of water.

Mathilde made a nearly convincing argument to make for the Mexican border but I had heard stories of other Americans being shot at the borders for assuming sanctuary. So we baked in the sun along with thousands of others, hoping somebody would take us to Tucson where Mathilde's brother waited for us. We hunted jackrabbits and skewered them over fires in emptied coffee cans. We collected moisture in bedsheets. Until finally, *finally*, a savior came in the form of a semi-truck driver working for a private company and, as long as we signed a waiver, we could hang on wherever we could find purchase outside the cargo hold.

The wind dehydrated us. I saw people grow weak and fall off into dirt and tires but I held steady onto Mathilde, who held steady onto our baby boy and I sold my soul, not to God or to Satan, but to her, to Mathilde, that we would see Tucson.

A storm hit us. We were rocked against riveted steel with the onslaught of rain coming down, slickening our grip, loosening my promises. I couldn't see who we lost in the storm. I just made sure that Mathilde's hand was in mine, and by the brief flashes of lightning, I could see that she was still there with me.

The storm passed when we found out that we had overshot Tucson by an entire town. On the west side of the country, though, hitching a ride was much easier. The reality of what happened in the east hadn't yet consumed the west coast and we were able to catch a ride with a noble fisherman, heading to Oregon by way of Phoenix, who said that Tucson was just far enough out of his way to give him something to do.

That man was an odd fellow. His name was Jackson Heit and he was assassinated in 1985, an hour after his nomination by the Voting Machine.

Anyway.

We made it to Tucson. Mathilde's brother, Edward, made us welcome, despite sharing the home with his wife and three kids. I had left my guitar out in the VW and had nothing to occupy my time so, as I said, I tried to write. Edward was nice enough to dust off an old Underwood and found me some paper so I could hone my craft on his back porch, smoking cigarettes instead of the usual joint. In retrospect, I think he did it to distract me instead of having to deal with the strange, traumatized man I had become.

I wrote three novels in the first month. Mathilde read them and burned them. I couldn't blame her.

Otherwise, life was nice. It became nice. Once I rehabilitated to family again, after I had exorcised the shit from my brain and onto the page—and after Mathilde had exorcised the shit on the page through the purifying altar of Edward's fireplace—I became present. We started participating in the community, learning to grow food, barter for what we didn't have and allow ourselves some happiness after our struggle. We were free. Mathilde and I were more in love than ever. My boy was growing up strong and we were making plans to make the hop to a place in California that hadn't been torn apart yet. Something north. Maybe Oregon, maybe eastern Oregon. But we were afraid of the party affiliations there and the strange rumors that began to proliferate around the region.

It didn't matter though. We were in love and we would've made anything work.

And then, right when I got my life back on track, I was nominated.

The Servicemen showed right up to Edward's door and asked for me. He asked for a warrant. Apparently, warrants were no longer a thing to be considered and they struck poor, generous Edward on the nose, knocking him down. Mathilde was inside with the kids and ushered them upstairs immediately.

The Servicemen found me on the back porch, enjoying the shade, as I typed the following sentence, riffing off a familiar poem:

"The Revolution will not be televised, but the apocalypse certainly will."

Which is either too clever by half or not clever at all. Either way, smug, as always, I sat back in my chair and chewed on my pen, grinning at the statement. In retrospect, it wasn't all that funny, but this was 1975. And it's also the last memory I had before a hood came down over my face.

The hood: an American flag ripped apart and sewn together. New American gauche.

There were a couple blows to the chest and I resisted at first until I felt the cold steel of a gun trace from my heart to my brain.

"Congratulations," someone said. "You're the first President of the New States of America."

I think I paused, not knowing what to say. It must've been 120 degrees under that face-sack. And I think I refused comment the rest of the ride, all the way to Omaha, Nebraska. When the Servicemen offered me water or food, I'd either nod or shake my head. If I nodded, a sweaty handed Serviceman would shove a piece of jerky in my mouth followed by a sip of water whenever I was done chewing.

You know, the royal treatment.

We stopped a couple of times and there was a slight shuffle around me. I asked what was going on and one of them told me that they were changing flags.

"Party affiliations," he clarified. "We don't want anyone to make us for Servicemen. We don't want anyone to know that we have you."

I asked, "How would anyone know who I am? I'm just some schmuck."

There was a pause and a laugh. Someone said, "He doesn't own a TV."

The rest of the drive went without incident and when the hood came off, we were in Omaha, Nebraska in front of a bleak, one-story building. The yellow paint was chipping off in huge flakes and you could still see where the words UNITED STATES POST OFFICE had been pried off the wall less than a year earlier.

I gestured, asking whether or not I should enter the building and my caretaker nodded, solemnly, more aware of the history we were making than I was. Praying for a meteor, I entered the building and let my hands slide against its barren walls, circling around its arid, dusty rooms and eventually sat down at a wobbly table in a broken chair.

From there, I'd make the most important decisions of the once-great nation of the United States of America. Aside from the annihilation of the coasts, and the creation of a totalitarian, panopticonical prison state, I'd like to think that I did an okay job of it.

Now, on to more pressing matters, 30 years later.

Pinball Politics

Riley Owen throws a Molotov cocktail through the glass window of the Frontmen's satellite office in Boise, Idaho. The bottle passes easily through the pane and connects with the front desk. She catches a glimpse of fire licking the walls before she breaks into a run, first down the street, and then across, sliding into an alleyway. She slows her gait as she approaches the dive bar. She takes a moment to hide the adrenaline-soaked look of pure glee from her face. The bar doesn't have a name but it's got a picture of a rifle crossed with a quilled pen burned in a slab of oak: Frontmen territory.

She enters and is sure not to look at the floor—that's the behavior of a suspect. She sees her boyfriend, Clay, over in the corner talking to two men playing pinball, each one nursing a mug of beer. She nods at Clay and gets herself a mug from the bar, pays cash (as cash is all there is anymore) and leans against the wall next to the men and their game. She's relaxed, for now, and lets Clay kiss her on the cheek.

"Boys," Clay says, "This is the gal I've been telling you all about."

"Yeah, we remember," says the guy on the pinball table. His friend is a little more cordial. He extends his hand.

"Xavier," he says. He points a thumb to the asshole playing pinball. "This's Reeve. Ya gotta forgive him. He's a little bent that I'm winning."

Reeve lets the ball drop below the flippers. He bangs on the table and swears. Xavier pats his back and takes over the machine.

"Come on, gimme something," Xavier prays to the table as he pulls back and releases the spring. Reeve finishes his beer in one swallow and lets his eyes flicker over Riley.

Still, he addresses Clay.

"So, what were you saying, man, about the *system*?"

Clay flicks his cap out of his eyes and wolfs a mouthful of beer down. He continues the story he'd been telling before Riley appeared.

"It's like this, right? We know there's a Voting Machine. At least, we think we know there's a Voting Machine. But what if, say, there wasn't?"

A waitress puts a fresh beer in front of Reeve. He doesn't thank her. He sips foam off the top.

"But there is. We know that," Reeve says, licking the foam from his lips.

"But what I'm saying," says Clay, "Is that there ain't no goddamn machine. The machine's a hoax. A prop of the old government, the old system that still chooses the top dog. The old money."

"Interesting," says Reeve. "But I don't buy it."

"That's RIGHT," yells Xavier to his pinball.

"Well, think about it," adds Riley. "It's the perfect ruse to distract the people from the common goal. I mean, look at the companies, the corporations, look at the people who still own the land, the dams, the means of production."

Reeve wags a finger and says, "So it's still all capitalistic. That wasn't necessarily the root of the problem."

Clay contends, "Let's say it wasn't—"

Reeve gulps beer and interrupts, "The problem was regulation and a lack thereof, goddammit! If we had sensible people—"

Riley's turn to interrupt: "If we had sensible people working for a damaged system, then those people are damaged."

"Sensibly damaged," adds Clay.

Reeve has more to say to this but Xavier's turn comes to an end in a swearing fit. Shortly after Reeve takes over the flippers, a man runs into the bar and screams:

"THE OFFICE HAS BEEN HIT."

Nearly all the patrons spring to their feet and pull out pistols. There's a chorus of interlocking steel pieces and the loading of cartridges into chambers.

Someone asks the exasperated man, "Any dead?"

"Not that I could see," he says, "But it's burned, it's burned out! It's a goddamn cavern!"

Reeve swears and hits Xavier to follow him out of the bar with everybody else to go check out the carnage.

That leaves Clay and Riley and a couple of elderly alcoholics alone in the bar.

"You get his keys?" Riley asks Clay.

"You betcha."

"Good boy."

They leave out the back, through an empty smoking patio, through another exit to the dumpsters. Parked on the gravel is a sleek, charcoal gray motorcycle.

"He called it the Reevemobile," snickers Clay. "What an ass."

They walk it out of the gravel into an alleyway, climb on, and Clay kicks it to a start. The Reevemobile takes off with a squeal. Avoiding the main drag, Clay sticks to side streets a while. Boise is dark at night—barely any streetlights remain functioning—and so it takes them a moment to get oriented. They figure out which direction is west and shoot for it, gunning the gas under the moonlight.

Throttling thunder behind them: a couple of Frontmen scouts on similar bikes. One whips back to alert the others, while one clings to their tail. They can't outrun it, Clay thinks, but if the road holds straight, they'll be able to at least stay in front until they get into friendlier territory. A bullet whizzes past Clay's ear. *So much for that theory.* Clay drops a gear and begins to serpentine. *If only there was oncoming traffic,* Clay thinks. *Too bad.*

The Frontmen scout has caught up to them and has a six shooter leveled at Riley's shoulder. She takes off one of her chain-link belts from a collection of old dog leashes, this one fastened with a padlock, and wraps it around her right hand. She taps Clay with her left and Clay squeezes the brake lever, closing the distance between them and the scout. The scout is about to put a round in them when Riley whips her chain into his helmet— the vizor cracks and the motorist appears a little dazed, but he's still on his bike. *And he's still got that damn gun,* Riley thinks. Another bullet whizzes by as Riley's chain-lock sparks, dangling against the pavement. She yanks it back up to see the scout lining up another shot. Clay hits the brakes again to get her close. Riley spins the chain along her side like a lasso, then looses it — the lock spins around the scout's handlebars. There's a microsecond of helmeted panic. And then Riley pulls hard.

Their pursuer eats pavement in a magnificent firework of sparks and broken bones. Riley drops her chain before it takes her with it and she and Clay speed off into the night, cackling like clowns, happy to be alive in this day and age.

Them Folk

Riley and Clay make it to the Oregon state border in just under an hour. Their plan is to head northwest and then loop back northeast to Spokane where the Scum operate. The Scum are friendly to the Dissent and it's about time you knew that Riley and Clay are classic Dissenters, fond of anarchy, monkey-wrenching other organizations, spreading confusion, and subverting any and all form of politics. The Scum, on the other hand—or wait, maybe it's the same hand, different finger—simply loved alcohol and life's finer powders. Spokane lies just half a day away, where whiskey and cocaine would welcome our destructive duo to their home away from home.

But, alas, the Reevemobile sputters and chokes and limps to the side of the road to die in the gravel. Clay kicks the handlebars.

"Out of gas! I don't believe it. We ran out of gas! I

thought those Frontmen guys had it together. But they don't even fill their tanks. Good Christ."

"Who can afford it?" asks Riley rhetorically.

Riley inspects the gas tank and places a finger on a jagged bullet hole. It pricks her finger and she sucks it, tasting blood and vaporous gasoline.

"The scout got us," she says.

Clay is crouching, holding his head and swearing into his cutoff jeans. "Maybe they did have it together," he muses.

Riley takes a look behind them. The road is clear and there's no sound of movement on the horizon—for now. The Frontmen probably found their scout and if he's alive he might've told the rest of them where Riley and Clay were headed. That, or they'd see the scout splattered on the pavement, note that he was chasing west, put two and two together and come this way, anyway.

Looks pretty grim, Riley thinks. She doesn't putz around like her partner and begins to drag the spent motorcycle off of the road. When Clay's tantrum subsides, he assists her in hiding the fallen Reevemobile into some brush.

Now where to hide themselves? Suffice to say there's not a whole lot for cover and as best as Clay can figure, it's at least a twenty mile hike across the desert to the adjacent highway.

He says, "We don't have the water to hike it."

Riley chimes, "If we do it now while it's night, we won't fry under the sun."

Clay says, "They'll find us anyway. They've got bikes

and trucks."

"They won't know we went off road if they don't find our bike."

"And if they do?"

Riley says, "They won't be stupid enough to drive off road at night."

"But we're stupid enough to hike it at night, is that it?"

"They won't expect it."

Clay says, "It's suicide."

Riley plants a smooch on Clay's mouth. She doesn't say anything else, she just starts walking. Clay lets her get a head start while he inspects the road. *Waiting here ain't any better, I guess.* Reluctantly, he plods along Riley's footsteps until he catches up with her.

Riley's got her eyes to the sky, taking in the desert starlight. Clay keeps on trying to start a conversation about something and she has to remind him to please shut the hell up and watch the night sky spin gently overhead.

"Actually, the stars are stationary," Clay says, "It's the earth that's moving."

"Shhhh…" hushes Riley. They're silent again and the only sound to be heard is the sound of Riley's dog chains (yes, she has more. She always has more.) quietly jangling against each other. She briefly thinks about ditching them, less weight to carry and all that, but that'd leave a trail to follow— and a specific one at that.

She imagines:

Hey, this is the same kind of chain link that yanked our

scout down to the ground.

Oh wow, you're right, chief. You think it's related to them folk we're chasing?

Could be. Could be.

Riley snaps out of it. She's dreaming. She wants to lie down and quit. The bags under her eyes try and grab for her eyelids and clamp 'em down, but she shakes her head out of it, turning her attention back to the stars above. Riley's a tough broad.

Clay's getting hungry. They hadn't packed for this. The plan had been to store up on snacks at a gas station once they were out of harm's way. *Gas station*, Clay silently fumes. *GAS STATION?!*

"What good is a gas station when you—"

"Shhhh."

But he can see the bright neon blue overhang and illuminated, exaggerated gas prices when he closes his eyes, that sweet oasis of licorice and jerky and beer, caffeinated drinks and little pebbled candies that come in a bag. Clay forgives the gas station as he imagines a benevolent dictator standing before a wall of cigarettes, welcoming him inside the store. *That's what the real America looks like. It's what it smells like.* Clay, at least in this moment, believes that a gas station is the most beautiful thing in the world because the thing about gas stations, is that they keep people *going*, no matter their cause.

Merchant mercenaries, he thinks, smiling broadly.

* * *

After five hours of walking, Riley is imagining the rings of Saturn groping Jupiter and she begins laughing. Clay imagines filling up a motorcycle with premium unleaded. The desert wind, albeit cold, has dehydrated them both and they are fatigued. Clay drops first, with the vision of rotisserie hotdogs clear in his mind's eye. Riley drops thirty paces further as she accepts Saturn's knowledge into her soul.

Day breaks and Riley licks her mouth. Chapped lips. No saliva. Clay thrusts awake, grasping for his junk food and is visibly upset when he doesn't find it.

"Y'all okay?" calls a voice.

Riley has to squint to find the source. The voice belongs to a white man with dreadlocks and loose corduroy pants and no shirt. Clay blinks and coughs.

"Yeah, we're okay," Riley calls back.

"You Frontmen?" Clay asks.

The man spits and says, "Hell no. I'm my own self. You bodies need a ride to town?"

Riley isn't so sure but Clay says, "There a gas station?"

"You betcha. Name's Vance. Nice to meetcha."

Riley and Clay climb into the back of Vance's truck. Vance gives them a gallon jug of water and climbs into the driver's seat. They get rolling until the desert turns to rocky hillside. The car turns south until they find a road. Clay can't quite orient himself. He pours some water on his head and then into his mouth. Riley accepts the jug from Clay and does the same. It feels like her fever boils the water away immediately. They look out to what they think is west for any pursuing vehicles, find none, and nestle into the truck bed, shielding their most sunburn-able parts.

The truck finally comes to a rest at a stoplight. Not that the stop light works anymore. It's just a formality. The engine revs and Riley and Clay are jumbled up once again in the bed until the truck reaches a stable 75 mph.

Silence in the bed. Too much wind to understand each other and not too much energy to speak anyway. In the cab, Vance is listening to the Grateful Dead at the highest volume his stereo can muster. The only thing to note overhead is the changing from an early, cloudy morning to a hell-sick, nightmarishly sunny noon. Riley and Clay fry. The jug's out of water. Clay hates himself for not stealing one of the Frontmen's canteens. Riley starts to question her involvement in the Dissent's purpose at all.

The truck makes a few more stops, hardly even California-rolls, until, after an hour, it comes to a rest and Vance kills the engine. Clay and Riley are mostly asleep in the bed. Vance pokes them both in the ankles with a hard finger.

Riley opens her eyes to a campsite—an entrenched one. Pop-tents are everywhere, littering three acres. A few of them are made from wood and pallets nailed together.

Clay says, "This ain't no gas station."

Vance says, "We hit the gas station. Tried to roust ya, but you were too far gone asleep. This here is Plentiville, Oregon. It's a nice little town we made ourselves. Us who don't take to the government sucking up our land, no matter's who's in charge. You hungry?"

Riley and Clay nod feebly and follow Vance to a campsite—or more accurately, a big black van covered in camouflage netting—and Vance introduces them to his family.

"There's my wife, Maggie, my son, Hunter, and there's my niece, Lucy." Vance points to a bent-backed, obese woman, a pudgy son, and a nettle-thin toddler, all with red hair, cooped under the shade of the netting. Vance strokes his graying dreadlocks, looking at his family with apparent pride before yelling, "Hey Maggie, these here were buzzard food! Howabout you make us all a stew and we get to know our new companions!"

The bent woman proceeds to heat some soup over a Sterno stove as Riley and Clay are seated in polyester camping chairs. Vance twists off the cap of some bourbon and passes it around.

"Good stuff, eh? Pre-New States. Ages well. It's got a picture of a bird on it. That's how you know it's fancy." He takes a pull from the bottle when it rounds back to him and he makes an exaggerated *ahhh* face after it hits his gullet. Vance is nice. Maggie is nice. Hunter and Lucy are children, not really paying any attention to anything except what's in front of their faces. And yet Riley feels unease. The whiskey helps, sure, but she can't help but feel that the onlooking townspeople rubbernecking her way meant that they hadn't quite reached a safe haven. One of those townspeople gets a little curious and sticks his head in under the net.

"Nice folk you got there, Vance. What're their names?"

Vance chases the man out, yelling, "These is mine people, hear me, Marshall?" And then he turns back to Riley and Clay, all smiles, speaking to Riley first.

"Sorry 'bout that. These folk in this town, they's good people. But they sure do like to ingratiate themselves in others' business."

The full force of the afternoon hits and Maggie serves her stew—modestly explaining that it was rabbit and onions, mostly—and Riley and Clay drink whiskey and water and lazily sit underneath the shade of the net. Clay falls asleep and Riley does too, but not before hearing Vance coo over their tired bodies, "Heat exhaustion. Every time, these people just get heat exhaustion."

In the sliver of Riley's waking eye, just before it clamps shut to the oblivion of sleep, she thinks she sees an elderly woman carry a basket of grapes across the campsite. The woman is wearing tattered clothing barely concealing the great girth of her belly. When she falls on the ground, the basket of grapes falls, too.

Except they aren't grapes, Riley thinks. They look almost like grapes but they aren't. They have irises. But then she thinks that must be the lunacy of a dream.

On The Tail

Xavier finds the Reevemobile in the dawn's meager light tucked under a shrub. Reeve nurses his ear, which has been freshly pierced with a star-shaped earring.

"I found it," Xavier calls over. Reeve curses incredulously until he sees his own motorcycle.

"Is it okay?" Reeve asks.

"Seems fine," Xavier says, examining the motor. "Just ran out of gas."

Xavier finds the bullet hole in the tank. Reeve swears again and paces, still holding his ear. His partner offers some condolences:

"Hey, it's not like they split your tongue or anything. You wear that for two weeks tops, pop it out and you'll be just as good looking as the rest of us."

I'll offer the explanation. The Frontmen's disciplinary system is based on body modification. Strike One gets you a pierced ear, or septum, or nipple, depending on the infraction. Strike two is a visible tattoo affiliated with an opposing party's ideologies. Strike three is brutal, but rare, in that either the tongue is split in two or piercings of the cheeks, nose-bridge, sternum, or lip are enforced. This is done to alienate the malcontent offender and force them to take on the appearance of enemy: the Dissent, the Scum, Enclavius Rex, and other anarcho-type gangs. Fellow Frontmen who knew the pariah would just laugh at him. But you put him in Frontmen territory in another state and now his safety is compromised by his own team.

Fun little trick, ennit?

But first infractions, the initial piercings, were only intended to put a little scare into the newcomers, and after two weeks, they were allowed to remove their earrings. Still, Reeve burns to the core, embarrassed. He kicks the motorcycle, sorry, the Reevemobile, in frustration. Xavier lets him be for the meantime and pulls from a canteen. Reeve huffs and pants.

He says, breathlessly, "What are you thinking. Where'd they go after they ditch the bike?"

Xavier looks to the pavement and says, "If it were me, I'd've walked along the road to a gas station. There's one maybe three miles north of here."

Reeve pants, "And not being you, not banking on that? What would you do?"

"What would you do?"

"If some folk were out to get me?"

"If some folk were out to get you," Xavier says.

Reeve says, "Then I would go west across this desert at night and hope to Christ that my pursuers wouldn't close in on me."

Both men look across the desert in front of them, imagine the work of tracking the footsteps and shudder in the heat.

Reeve turns to Xavier and says, "What were you saying about a gas station?"

Xavier kicks a rock into another rock. "That there's one a couple miles north of here."

"I mean, there's a few in the area. I'm saying, if they went west, they would've hit a road."

"Which means they might've been picked up by a car."

Reeve says, "...And filled up on gasoline."

"It ain't much," Xavier says.

Reeve says, "It's a start."

"It's bupkis."

"Bupkis is better than shit," Reeve says, "There's a hierarchy." He jumps into the driver's side of the marked Frontmen truck.

"Is there?" Xavier mutters before getting in the passenger seat. They're a few miles up the road before Xavier reminds Reeve of his motorcycle, and there's a round of cursing, and the truck spins around and guns to the shrub.

They lift the motorcycle into the bed of the truck, slam the gate shut and get on their way again.

Wild eyed, Reeve punches the gas pedal and kicks up huge plumes of dust as the truck rockets up the road.

They reach the first gas station in a matter of minutes. Xavier, carsick from Reeve's driving, is eager to get out of the truck again. Their visit doesn't last long, however, as the gas attendant hasn't seen a single customer for two days. They get their truck filled with unleaded, filling up the Reevemobile too (placing it back in the truck bed, carefully, after wedging a rubber cork in the bullet hole), and each get a candy bar and a soda, which they eat and sip back in the truck.

The next gas station is 40 minutes away and the radio isn't working. Xavier hums along to a song he'd heard at the bar the night before. Reeve is able to take it for 3 minutes and 17 seconds before he explodes into furious annoyance. This is often the dynamic between Xavier and Reeve. They could be brothers, if only Reeve shared Xavier's blond hair and ditched his perma-scowl.

The second gas station is a bust and worse, offers a crossroad that splits north and south. They eat ice cream on the curb trying to decide on a course of action.

"We should split up," Reeve says.

Xavier licks melty ice cream from his fingers. "Hell no. We split up and we run into them? Then it's two against one. And that's *assuming* it's just the two of 'em."

"Fine then. Where's the next nearest gas station?"

Xavier thinks a moment as he begins to chew on the cone. "North."

"Fine, north it is."

They drive with the windows down. It's another hour to the nearest gas station and this one pays off. The gas attendant gives a description of a green truck that passed through with "kind of a fat fellow at the wheel, kind of hippie-ish," and "a gal in chains and a skinny man in the back." The attendant spits chewing tobacco. "They's kind of dirty, too. Just as well they didn't stop to buy nothin'."

"Which way did they go?" Reeve asks, his voice flecked with borderline-terrifying determination.

The gas attendant points to a road. "Now, you boys buyin' anything?"

Reeve is already out the door towards the car. Xavier shrugs and joins his partner.

At the wheel, Reeve nearly foams at the mouth.

"If we find them, you know what that means for us?"

"You get that stupid earring out, at the very least."

"Yes! And depending on what kind of information they give us, who they're affiliated with, other plans of subterfuge, you know, that could mean a lot for us. That could mean we climb the ranks."

"No more errand fetching." Xavier smiles, but only for a moment. He says, "But then, maybe we'd no longer be partners."

"Oh, I cannot WAIT!" Reeve guns the engine.

In twenty minutes they reach the entrance to a shanty town, seemingly built on top of nothing. Reeve gets out first and asks a little girl on a tricycle if they'd seen a green truck come back here in the last 36 hours. The girl doesn't say anything. Xavier gets out of the car and gives her a dollar. She pouts. Xavier sighs and puts another dollar in her hand. The girl cheerfully points over to some shade netting with a van and a truck parked next to it. A woman is tending to some stew while a large, graying, dread-headed man dozes in a camping chair. A suspicious lump of blankets lies on a couch.

"Beat it, kid," says Reeve following the lead. Xavier follows.

They stop just outside the netting opening. Xavier pops his head in first.

"Pardon us," Xavier says. The large woman turns around and greets them happily.

"Oh, hello! Who're you boys, now? New neighbors?"

"No, we're not your new neighbors. I'm Xavier and this is Reeve."

"Maggie," Maggie says as she extends a hand. "You hungry? There's plenty."

Reeve pulls on his knuckles.

Xavier says, "No thank you, ma'am. We're looking for a young couple."

Reeve adds, "A few friends of ours went missing last night. We think they might've gotten lost."

It's usually best to let Xavier do the talking. He's more of a people person and thinks quickly on his feet, occasionally *too* quickly. Reeve is more of a deck of cards and a bottle of whiskey kind of person. He gets angry and frustrated easily, but he can work a con and say the right things when the right things need to be said. But that doesn't hide his deep-seated fury. Right now, he's eyeballing the sleeping man with obvious contempt.

The woman responds, "A couple, you say? Well, that doesn't narrow things down. You see, people come and go from our little town as they please."

"Is that right?" Reeve asks.

"God's truth," Maggie answers. "I might've seen some folk come in, but I can't say anyone stood out. What'd they look like?"

Through gritted teeth, Reeve says, "There was a girl who wore black and green and a lot of chains. Dog chains. Some with padlocks. The man was skinny, wore blue jeans and a vest and a cap." He looks like he's going to pop a nerve out of his forehead. Maggie shakes her head.

"No... that don't sound familiar at all. I'm not really the person to ask about this, sweetie, truth be told. I'm usually right here, cooking somethin' or another."

"Did *he* see anyone?" says Reeve, through teeth, jerking his head at the sleeping fat hippie.

Xavier covers. "Do you think we could wake up your husband, ma'am? Ask him some questions, too?"

Maggie smiles. "By all means, boys."

Right on cue, Vance yawns and sits up. Reeve is suspicious that he was ever asleep to begin with.

"Afternoon," Vance says. He coughs out some mucous and asks Maggie to put on some coffee. To the Frontmen, he asks, "What's yer business, boys? You affiliated?"

"We're Frontmen," says Xavier. Reeve jabs him in the ribs.

"Frontmen, eh? Well, I'll be. That's the one that wants

to reinstall regulation, huh? Big govvie, just like before?"

"That's the one," says Reeve, ready for a fight.

Xavier saves the day. "We're not here to argue, sir."

Vance sniffs. "Well, I ain't affiliated with nobody 'cept my family and Plentiville here. I guess it don't bother me none that you boys got ideals. So, what d'ya need from me?"

"Um," stutters Reeve.

Xavier says, "We're looking for a couple. Boy and a girl. Dark clothes, lotsa makeup on the gal. Chains, too."

"Friends of yours?"

Xavier: "Best friends."

"They don't dress like Frontmen."

Xavier: "They don't affiliate."

Reeve: "We bicker about it constantly."

Vance eyes them warily. He let his shoulders drop and says, "Sure. I picked up a couple of hitchhikers yesterday morning, 'round the Jewel gas station. Took 'em here to give 'em some water and drove 'em down to the 20, so they could hitch a ride to Bend."

"That was yesterday?"

"Yesterday morning, very early, yessir."

"Goddammit."

Reeve asks, "They say what their destination was?"

"No. I'd figure Klamath Falls, though, 'less they bang on further down south."

Reeve swears and locks his hands behind his head. Xavier claps a hand on his shoulder. Maggie makes an offer of stew and only Vance obliges (rude of them not to accept, doncha think?) and Xavier and Reeve make back for their truck. Empty handed.

Xavier drives. Reeve bitterly chews his thumbnail and stares out the window.

"We were so close," Reeve mutters.

Their radio explodes into static, startling them both. A frantic voice comes through in shouts and white noise.

"B—NNY—GR——RE—DE-D."

Reeve grabs the mic.

"Do not copy. What was that? Over."

"BENNY-GREERE-IS-DEAD," the voice shouts. Xavier furrows his brow.

"Who's Benny Greere?"

"Copy that," Reeve says. "Who's Benny Greere? Over."

"-E-WAS-TH-PR—S-DENT."

Reeve pauses. "What? Over?"

"THE PRESIDENT," the voice shouts. Reeve and Xavier look at each other. Reeve puts his seatbelt on as Xavier floors the gas pedal.

Life on the Farm

Riley careens back and forth, attempting to topple her cage. Her hope is that the cage is poorly constructed and that the welded iron bars will break from the iron platform the bars are welded to, if she only applies enough aggressive entropy. Her cage is covered in burlap. She can't see much and her fear is that she is in plain sight of one these godforsaken hippie cannibals. She compares the wailing and moaning of her fellow captives to the general peace of silence of the campsites she witnessed in Plentiville and figures that these holding cages must be *out of the way*. She rocks on.

Riley succeeds, and perhaps overachieves, in that she was able to shift the weight of her cage such that it falls on its side intact. Dust coughs into the burlap sack. Riley holds back tears as well as her breath. She holds back from cursing loudly as she silences the pain received from slamming her head into three iron bars against the ground. She gains focus and calms herself down. She's contorted sideways. Can she turn around? Yes, it *turns* out, as she twists onto her back, taking her time making her legs cooperate with the spatial constraint. Can she see? A little better than before, as the tumble caused a rip in the burlap. Can she use her hands? No, not quite, as her wrists are bonded with plastic cable ties. Can she break those ties against the iron bars? The answer is yes, but it takes a little while. She tries gnawing on it with her teeth and makes no progress except chipping her enamel a little. She gives up, throwing her wrists at the bars (a hard feat in a confined space) over and over again until the plastic catches on a barb of rust. Flat out ruins her knuckles, which also catch on the iron. Blood trickles onto her face during the effort. Eventually, the cable tie gets a scratch which turns into a wedge which then turns into a clean break after Riley presses it into one of the bars above her and it snaps. Riley takes a break, panting.

What's next?

Next, Riley takes an inventory of what she's got on her person. She's got a lighter (although her captors took her marijuana and cigarettes), her wallet (although her captors have taken her meager sum of bills), and a spent tube of chapstick (as chapstick hasn't been manufactured in a couple of years). Riley grips the bars in frustration. As tears well up in her eyes, she hears a jangle. *Chains.* They've left the dog chains that Riley wears around her waist (usually three, now two after the motorcycle chase), and around her neck (just the one, because she's classy), as well as the dog leash she has wrapped around her ankle up to her knee, over her jeans (purely for aesthetic value).

Riley gathers herself, removes a chain from her waist and loops it through the iron bars above her. She takes both ends in hand, pulling her face into her shoulder and yanks down. She hears a squeak— a minor fissure of the welding. She tries again, but can't recreate the noise. She figures her problem is leverage. *If only her cage was upright again.* Riley begins throwing her weight up at the cage such that it could right itself. The burlap covered cage can't seem to plant itself where it once stood again. Exhausted, Riley loops the chain around one bar above her, wraps it around one bar to her left, faces the opposite direction and pulls with all of her weight. Her back and shoulders bruise against the added pressure.

The sound of welded iron peeling off iron doesn't sound like much to people like you and me. It sounds like *skrgnt*. To Riley, it sounds like hope. Or if not hope, then the postponement of certain death via butchery. She would've wept with joy, if only she wasn't absolutely terrified of being discovered. She moves onto bar number two. *Skrgnt.* And three. *Skrgnt.* You might get the picture. When all the bars are bent inward to the cage, she's able to use her legs to push 'em outward. Not far, maybe a foot or so. That's enough to squeeze out of, if you don't mind the iron claw marks on your stomach, legs and ass. Which Riley didn't— at this particular time.

Once out of the cage, and out of the burlap sack covering the cage, she returns the iron jail to its standing position, making sure that the burlap sack is still covering it, hiding the torn seam. She takes a look around. There are dozens of cube-shaped burlap sacks, nearly all of them crying, in what appears to be a dried up gulch. Riley keeps low, passing one sad sack after the other. She pops her head up to see a sign—a spray painted piece of corrugated steel— that reads "THE FARM." Next to the sign: a fat teenager holding a shotgun, not paying much attention to anything but his own imagination. It's not hard to evade him. Riley just keeps to the outermost cages and slinks away, away from the fat kid, away from the cubes, down the dried riverbed until everything is out of sight.

She's free. She ambles up the hill and hides behind a shrub, thankful for the gift of fresh desert air. She's *free.* That takes a moment to set in. It's just usually taken for granted. When it isn't, it's understood comparatively.

Riley says it, whispering the words. *"Free."*

But there's a pang of regret: Clay. Clay will be stew meat if she doesn't do something. Whiny, gangly sonuvabitch though he may be, she cares for him, and even though death was an assumed resolution to their philosophy, she'll be damned if he's gonna be eaten by goddamn hippie savages.

From the brush, Riley can see the camp about half a mile off. She sees that it's set up in a time-forgotten lakebed, where an ancient glacier settled and died. Her first impulse is to sneak into the camp, steal some guns and knives and then have the fat teenage bastard cut her boyfriend loose... a fine, clandestine fantasy, free from human error. But Riley's adrenaline screams for results. *Results, dammit.* Rational outcomes are often born out of desperate need.

It's not like she could just break his cage like she had done with hers. There's nothing to push against, no leverage to break the bars. And if she could, she doesn't know which cage is his. Half of a plan forms in her head. She decides to ride the adrenaline rush and slinks along through the shadows back to the cages.

Whereas, at first, her tactic of escape was discretion, her design to save Clay is predicated on the exact opposite. She unravels a dog leash and takes a deep breath. She whips the chain, striking the iron bars of all of the cages in her vicinity. When the sobs turn into frightened shrieks, Riley runs, ducking between burlap, keeping her head low.

Riley screams, "I'm free! I'm free!"

If the shrieking prisoners hadn't gotten the teenager's attention, this surely does. Riley sees him adjust his hat before jumping off his stool, which falls behind him into the dust. He fires a shot into the air and hustles to see what the commotion is all about.

Great, Riley thinks. *The Plentivillians are gonna send back up. Better make this quick.*

She keeps out of the teenager's line of sight, flanking him. He's pounding on cages and telling the prisoners to shut up.

"You best quit that racket, unless you want a belly full of buckshot," he yells.

That brings the shrieking down to a simper. The distraction works. Riley is able to get close behind the boy. He's looking around, eye flush to sights, but it never occurs to him to look behind until too late.

When he sees her, he's too confused to shoot. Riley whips her chain down across the gun and yanks it out of his hands. As she does this, there's a moment of very real panic in her stomach that the boy might turn and clutch the trigger, her head popping off like a balloon full of spaghetti.

Luckily for her, the gun falls harmlessly to the ground. She rushes to claim it, as does the portly teenager. He tries to push her face away, but her head is too slick with her own blood and his hands slip. She lands a punch right in his right kidney and he doubles over, wasting seconds nursing it. She grabs the shotgun, pumps the action, shakes the dirt out of the barrel against her boot, and levels it at the teenager's head. He wets himself.

"Keys," Riley demands. The boy produces a cartoon smiley-face keychain with a single key on it. He offers it to her.

"Don't give that to me."

The teenager nods several times in apology.

"That work for every cage?"

The teenager nods.

"Crack one open," Riley demands.

"If they run away, we'll starve!"

"Well, you should have thought about that before you started eating people. Open up. Come on."

He whimpers and obeys, lugging one knee up after the other. He throws off a burlap sack and frees a padlock. A boy about the same age as him pops out gasping for air. When he's fully oxygenated, his eyes correct and fall on the teenager.

"Clark?" he pants, incredulously. "You complete—*wheeze*— and utter bastard!" The freed boy jumps out of the cage and onto Clark and begins wailing on him with his fists. Riley allows this. Clark is rendered unconscious quickly. The boy gets off of the teenager and stretches his back. He eyes the girl with the shotgun suspiciously, but relaxes when he sees her bleeding knuckles.

"You freed me?" he asks.

Riley nods.

"Thanks. I'm Cam."

"Riley."

"Pleasure."

Cam frisks Clark for a pocket knife and starts slashing open bags. Riley follows and removes the padlocks.

"We gotta go quickly," she urges Cam. "More of these sick lunatics are coming."

The people they free are confused and scared. Many recognize Cam and have brief, heartfelt reunions with him. Of course, some of the people in the cages are dead, but I don't want to focus too much on that. It's kind of a bummer and degrades the luster of Cam and Riley's heroic moment.

Once they start to gather, Riley urges everyone to flee. Some do, some huddle together, either from shock or from frostbite. Cam finishes slashing open the remaining bags as Riley follows until she opens the last padlock, hoping to see Clay's stupid, living face beam back at her.

Nope. Just a crying old man. Riley deflates, flummoxed and disappointed.

I guess they ate him.

There's not a lot of time to mourn as the freed captives spot a dust cloud forming on the horizon. Cam runs to see what it is. His suspicions are confirmed. The people of Plentiville heard the shotgun blast and the ensuing violence; Plentiville is sending its backup in the form of a pickup truck full of well armed cannibals. Riley scouts for cover. There's a slightly mountainous area not too far off— maybe a mile and a half away. It'd be hard to travel though there with a vehicle— if they left now they'd have a chance to escape. Riley tells this to Cam.

"I ain't budging."

"But they're gonna kill us and eat us!" Riley says.

"They might. But there's a lot more of us than there are of them," Cam replies.

"I'm staying, too!" another shouts. Then another. And another. United together, the band of prisoner-stew-meats decides to stay and fight. They've got a vendetta to settle. Riley doesn't. Riley looks at the shotgun in her hands and passes it over to Cam. She also gives away one of her waist chains to the hardiest young man she can find.

"Swing high," she tells him. "Before swinging low."

She salutes Cam. "I'm sorry I can't stick around."

"You set us free. You done enough. This is our fight now."

And with that, Riley breaks into a jog, out of the gulch and towards the rocky scree. She hears the clamor of war behind her. Gun shots and screams. She likes to think Cam and his meager army of starved prisoners gave the cannibals of Plentiville what-for.

But she doesn't look back, lest she turn into a pillar of salt, or more accurately, a bullet-riddled corpse.

The Dragon Rears its Head

Well, what a mare's nest Riley has got herself in there, huh? And apparently out of. Good for her.

Reeve and Xavier, they sure have a whole lot on their plate too, what with the information on the dead President, and I ain't talking slang for a single dollar bill. Of course, most old dollar bills these days are defaced beyond recognition, no one really seems to know what George Washington's face looks like. Well, I remember. He looks like a cotton-mouthed clown with no makeup. I'm not wrong, either. These days, they got my own smiling portrait on all their bills. That's right, Clyde O'Brien smiling at the masses, masking his own suffering. But I guess the world chooses its heroes to suit the times, don't it?

Shame they had to pick me.

So let's talk about me. Satisfy that curiosity of yours. I

suppose I am somewhat of a hero, depending how you want to look into it. Let's talk about that first year of the New America, with me sitting in office.

But first, let's start with the fact that since 1975 there have been 21 Presidents of the New States and 113 assassinations. A paradox? Not really. Only 21 served the full year term. Only 4 were killed during that term. The rest of the 109 occurred immediately after the mathematical nomination, right before serving. You see, after a spell of this rehabilitative Presidency program, some folk took to murdering the leader and keeping things unstable. But them Servicemen do a damn fine job and it got harder and harder to kill the leader of the New States. So someone had the bright idea to kill the poor bastard before he reached office, or, even better, before the Servicemen could claim him and indenture him (or her. We've had 11 women as serving presidents. 47 would-bes). As you can imagine, this *impeachment* process implied grand schemes of manipulation. If the President of the New States is elected completely at random, meaning that *anybody* could be elected, it follows that *anybody* in a *specific political affiliation* could take the reins. Hence the many assassinations. That's why Reeve and Xavier were so keen to hotstep back to their scorched headquarters. They needed to figure out who Benny Greere was, who he was affiliated with, and keep on the line to figure out who was next elected. If it wasn't Frontmen, they'd get a location, flank and kidnap the poor bastard (The Frontmen weren't quite as murderous as their competitors, but nonetheless cruel with their persuasive implements). It could be anybody, anywhere. If it was a Frontman, which hasn't happened yet, despite being one of the largest "liberal" groups in America, they'd locate him or her, flank, defend and retreat to the nearest headquarters. Gang politics.

But you don't want to hear about rules and trends, do ya? You want to hear about ole Clyde O'Brien's big day in the oval office— suffice to say that the office was not an oval, mind you, but rather square and drab, with the sound of running water constantly flowing somewhere behind the walls.

Well, let me start by telling you that being President is absolute horse shit. That old Post Office became my home. There's a cot in the basement that the Servicemen are cheeky enough to refer to as "the Pleasure Suite." There's just the cot and a meager library of US history books, intended for your basic retarded child in third grade. And there's some science books in there, too, sure, but they've gone and ripped all the pages out that had to do with the dinosaurs or anything alluding to an earth that wasn't 6,000 years old. There was also the Bible and, somewhat scandalously, the complete works of Shakespeare. How I came to adore Shakespeare! Magnificient bard! Thou'st sav'd this poor boy! I'd read Macbeth and scoff as its comparative simplicity.

There was no kitchenette or refrigerator. Meals were dictated by the house chef, a cruel woman who served nothing but ground beef and carrots on Sundays, and fetid gruel the rest of the week. The one accommodation allowed in the office was a coffee machine; however, the grounds were rationed and spared and the coffee itself looked like bilge water and tasted none better. To be fair, the Servicemen would occasionally give me a cigarette (but no weed) and on Christmas they smuggled me a piece of cornbread, two strips of bacon, and a beer.

I was allowed outside only in the fenced yard. I never thought I'd consider Omaha, Nebraska a beautiful sight, but I did. I could see the city, or the hints of a city, by the lights off at a distance and that was my go-to reassurance that I hadn't somehow thrown our country into the hopper. Omaha would shine for me then. But then, in the yard, I could see the plains upon plains and the highways that slit 'em up sideways and I'd think *this was such a beautiful place before we set our hammers to it.* A Serviceman would remind me that I was needed to make a decision about something and then I was ushered back inside.

There was one such occasion where I was infatuated with the scene of a raccoon feeding its family when a strong-armed lady pulled me away and shoved me back into my seat. A memo sat on my desk. We don't talk about the poetry of memos enough. A thousand hours goes into information-gathering, I was told, by hundreds of Servicemen affiliates. They had provided a two lined memo on my desk.

RUSSIANS INVADING WASHINGTON STATE

CORRIDOR
EXPECTING EXECUTIVE ORDER

Well, I knew the Army was still intact in the diminished form of a Servicemen wing. I said, "Line it up from Washington to Maine."

The resulting memo asked, "WITH SOLDIERS?"

And I replied, "If ya got 'em."

Which was interpreted as, line the northern border with mines, line the southern border with mines, line the east coast border with mines, and while you're at it, line the west coast border with mines. I balked when the memo was received. I was halfway done typing through my response when another memo arrived.

DC NUKED

Cold sweat and tears ran down my face as I loaded another page into the type writer. Another memo was recieved:

SAN FRANCISCO NUKED

I typed furiously, trying to come up with a plan. I got as far as emergency evacuation of several major cities. Another memo came.

SEATTLE PORTLAND LA

I passed out. A Serviceman shook me back awake. With another memo.

NYC BOSTON

I crumpled it up and looked out the window. It was serene, my little window to the world. It looked like nothing nuclear could ever happen to it. And yet, I was given another memo. This one read:

DELIVER NUCLEAR PAYLOAD

I wrote a song once called "The Grifter" about how corporate entities had sucked the soul from Americans' eyes and replaced it with nationalistic hatred. I had a line in there about putting down our weapons, and embracing one another like true brethren. Weapon, brethren. That was the rhyme. I wrote a memo back. It said:

SURE.

They wrote back and asked: WHERE.

I gave two locations. I'm not saying which.

I went outside to smoke a cigarette and calm my nerves under the sun. More memo cards piled up on my desk, telling of disastrous strikes on American soil. I ignored them and paced around, trying not to think of the words Mutually Assured Destruction. The memos stopped around dusk and I took out a map of The United States and started marking off destroyed cities. The entire West Coast was gone. So was the Northeast, and most of the East Coast all the way down. Florida was fine. *Of course.*

A Serviceman interrupted me and told me that I needed to give the American people a speech. I wasn't very much prepared. I sat at my desk, sweaty and disheveled, as a video camera was set up. I don't remember what I said. I think it went something like...

"My fellow Americans this is Clyde O'Brien, your president. Today we've been dealt a heavy blow by our enemies. We struck back in due fashion and they won't catch us again vulnerable. We mourn our dead and the loss of our cities. But America goes forward, in great strides, despite this titanic loss. I assure you that we'll get through this dark period and see the dawn's light shine on us once again. And I put it to you at home to step up, put down your weapons and embrace your brethren. We need the union to stand strong now more than ever. United we stand."

When the cameras were off, I bawled like a baby and went to bed and slept for two days. When I finally shuffled back upstairs to that grim desk, I was given a report of what was considered irradiated and what was not. I then went back to the map I was drawing and drew an outline of untainted America. It looked like a dragon's head facing east.

I wrote an executive order to fence this dragon head off with high, concrete walls to be defended by whatever remained of the military wing of our Servicemen.

I went back to sleep and woke up to lesser issues, gradually. The riots, the violence, nothing could shake me more than the nuclear annihilation of half the country. I served out the remainder of the year like this, completely numb. Sleeping often.

Until finally, it was time for me to return home to Tuscon to my wife and son and brother-in-law, which happened promptly and secretively and without ceremony.

As far as anyone can figure out, I was shot and killed by a platoon of the Just immediately after the Servicemen left me alone.

Dumb Luck

Clay doesn't know how lucky he is. He wakes up from a long nap on the polyester couch in Plentiville. The sky is gray and the air is heavy with chilled dew. Vance sips coffee with his feet up on a cooler.

"Mornin' sunshine," Vance says with a wide grin. "Sleep well?"

Clay yawns and scratches himself. "Not too bad. Boy, it's cold, huh?"

"Warm yourself up with some java, my man."

Clay accepts a warm aluminum mug of coffee and sips slowly, blinking his eyes quickly in order to shake the sleep from his lids. The coffee burned his throat and he spluttered and coughed.

He asks, "Where's Riley?"

Vance smiles and wraps a gray dreadlock around his finger. "That gal you was with? Welp, when night came down some boys offered to drive her over to Spokane. She took the offer."

Clay gulps his coffee, burning his throat. "She left me here?"

Vance shakes his head. "Afraid to tell ya, son. We were going to wake you, but she said she was better off alone."

This takes a moment to sink into Clay's rather thick skull. Vance takes the opportunity to again inspect the meat on Clay's bones and shakes his head. *Too stringy*, thinks Vance. *Not worth the food and water to keep him alive.*

Panic flows into Clay's throat. He says, "What am I supposed to do?"

Vance slaps the dust from his feet. "That's up to you, son. Could be that there's more folk heading to Spokane and you'd probably be more 'an welcome to join 'em. We, uh, ain't equipped for permanent tenancy here, understand?"

Clay nods and furrows his brow. "Right. Sure. And people drive to Spokane often?"

Vance shrugs. "Sometimes they do. I suppose you could always go back the way you came."

Clay remembers the gang of Frontmen chasing him and Riley out of Boise. He laughs, noticeably uneasy. "I think I'll try for Spokane," he says. But he doesn't move. "Maybe I can stay for lunch."

"Sure ya can," says Vance, joylessly.

Clay hangs around until past two in the afternoon, lounging around Vance's campsite. He makes small talk with Maggie. They talk about the weather. ("It sure got hot in a hurry!") He eats a bowlful of stew, or tries to, anyway. For whatever reason, he can't stomach more than two bites before retching. *It's the heat,* he thinks. The poor sap. He drinks water and helps tidy up the campsite. ("Gotta do my campsite dues!") Vance's cheeriness diminishes quickly. In fact, it's just about plum depleted by the time Clay comes back from the kybo.

Vance says, "Son, I think it's time you were on your way."

Clay, unaware of when he's overstaying his welcome, says, "Sure thing, Boss. It's pretty warm right now, though. I think I'll make better time hitching once the afternoon is over."

Vance tightens his grip on a carving knife. Maggie gives him a stern look. Vance releases his grip and attempts a smile. "Mi casa, su casa."

Clay takes a nap in a hammock until 4 in the afternoon. Vance decides to chop Clay's head off with an axe and feed him to the "Farm Animals." *Oh yes, I've had enough,* Vance thinks, *who's going to have a problem with it? There's a general no murder rule here in Plentiville, but we EAT people for Chrissakes! He's not one of us, either! He's an outsider! No one knows his family! It'll feel so good, it'll make me feel better, it'll be a real fun time,* Vance thinks, a glint of cheer returning to his eyes. He's on the verge of carrying out the dirty deed, just about to get up and walk over to his trunk where his wood chopping axe lay next to a small hatchet (*axe for the head, hatchet for the limbs*), when Clay springs up, scratches his back and yawns. Clay shakes Vance's hand and thanks him for everything before leaving camp and hitching up the highway. Vance is nearly stunned and finds the chores around his campsite to be incredibly tedious without the omnipresent intrusion of Clay and those invasive, murderous thoughts to distract him.

"Well I'll be damned," muses Vance, chuckling slightly. "I think I'll miss the kid." Vance shakes his head and returns to peeling potatoes for the next pot of people stew. Someone runs past him armed with a shotgun. And then another person.

"Our cattle's loose!" cries one of the runners. Vance considers joining the men with his own weapon but instead remains in his chair, peeling potatoes and dimly considers whether or not Plentiville has changed him and Maggie for the worse. *Something's definitely different.* He frowns and peels potatoes.

Clay, meanwhile, makes it to the highway in fairly decent spirits. Although apparently abandoned by his girlfriend, Clay reflects that he'd been left before and he'd be left again and that there is no point wasting time feeling heartbroken. There is no assaulting this kid's self esteem. You could tell him his face was made out of the porous anus of a walrus and he would write you poetry about the brininess of the sea. Whether or not this makes Clay an idiot, a sociopath, or a thick skinned hero to all of us who suffer from the afflictions of self-doubt and hesitation remains rather debatable. Option D; all of the above.

It is probably this bubbly attitude that appeals to the fifth car, a rusty hatchback, that passes Clay on the highway and, impressed with his upbeat optimism (a rarity in America, much less for a member of the Dissent), pulls over to offer Clay a ride to none other than Spokane, Washington— the "Ceiling of America," and the hometown of the Scum.

As it turns out, the people in the car are Scum members. Their names are Cody and Carly and they have an unique number of nitrous oxide canisters. Clay feels at home as Cody shoots the hatchback north.

Impotent Anger

Xavier and Reeve stand at the bar watching the television screen along with a dozen other Frontmen. Gary Denilles, the mathematician is onscreen next to his electoral calculating machine. He is dressed soberly in black and white and carries out the night's duties with sober eloquence.

Denilles says to the viewers, "As you know, Benny Greere, our beautiful nation's previous candidate was found murdered by a political group known as the Truth Bearers." The image of Denilles flickers and his words fuzz out slightly. Someone in the bar complains about the signal quality, followed by the command to 'shut up.'

Denilles says, "It is my duty, as you know, to operate the Voting Machine and pick another presidential candidate. If your name is chosen, it is highly recommended that you barricade yourself inside and wait for the Servicemen to find you. It is for your safety— and the safety of your family— that you comply fully to the needs of the Servicemen. I repeat, you must comply fully with the Servicemen."

Xavier tightens a screw on his modified .45, before looking down the barrel with one eye.

"Hogwash," he says. "I bet you the Servicemen are just as likely to kill a candidate as we are, if they don't like his ideals."

Reeve is tense. He doesn't care for this ritual too much. He'd rather be playing pinball. But there's an element of duty here, to protect a Frontmen candidate, should one get called. Beads of sweat condense on Reeve's brow and his pits are soaked. His hands keep occupied playing with a flint lighter. The *click* and *snap* of the lighter goes ignored by Xavier, who usually abhors the noise. On screen, Denilles fiddles with his machine before pulling a comically sized lever. A long number rolls into place, but the screen is too fuzzy for Reeve or anyone else to make out. The machine calculates who the number belongs to as Denilles narrates about as much to the audience. Finally:

"Nicholas Somner," says Gary Denilles, looking straight into the camera. "Nicholas Somner, please stay inside and await the Servicemen to aid you to Omaha. Thank you, America." The screen goes dark as the bartender turns the knob. The noise level is chaotic and Reeve's eyes dart around the room, trying to trace the commotion and figure out what was going to happen next. Reeve calls for quiet.

A short man in glasses opens a book, the Frontmen directory, that has the records of everyone affiliated with the Frontmen. If Nicholas Somner was a Frontman, they'd find him here.

"Sommers, Sommerset, Somner..." whispers the bald man, tracing a finger down the directory. "Somner, Mathew...Nathan... Nicholas? ..."

The bald man stays quiet for a moment.

"Is he one of ours?" begs someone. The bald man takes off his glasses.

He says, "He's one of ours. Right here. Nicholas Somner. Address listed is in... Utah. Salt Lake."

"That's not too far from here," Xavier says, smiling and jabbing Reeve in the ribs. "Bet we could make it in three hours if we really hauled ass."

"Great," mutters Reeve.

"Okay, everyone," yells a dapper young Frontman standing on top of the bar. "One of ours has been elected President! This could mean big things for the Frontmen! But first we need to make it down to Salt Lake City and protect our newly elected official!"

Xavier cups his hands to mouth and shouts, "Who're we up against in Utah?" The dapper young man points back to Xavier in response.

"Good question. Marcus, who's in Utah?"

The bald man, Marcus, opens a different, smaller notebook and flips through a couple of pages of notes, crossed out scribbles, and crammed annotations in various colors of ink.

"There's a chapter of Frontmen there, Chapter 217." Cheers from the crowd at the confirmation of of their Frontmen brethren. Marcus squints.

He says, "Primary political party of the area is..."

"Spit it out," Xavier mutters.

"The Angels of Prophecy," says Marcus and a wave of relief passes through the room. The Angels of Prophecy aren't militarily active, being more of an ineffectual charity group with occasional outbursts of spiritualistic criticism.

Xavier slaps Reeve on his back and says, "That's a shame, right? I was getting excited for some action, there."

Reeve swallows hard and tells Xavier to be quiet. Marcus is still examining his notebook.

Reeve sees Marcus mouth the words, "Oh dear." Reeve is sweating like cheese in the desert. The dapper young man calls everyone to share quiet.

"I'm afraid I mispoke," says Marcus. "As of Febuary of last year, the Angels of Prophecy were rousted from their headquarters in Salt Lake City and the Just installed themselves as the city's primary political party." Marcus closes his book and holds it with clasped hands in front of him. He adds soberly, "Chapter 217 of the Frontmen was dismantled by the Just in April of this year."

Faces dour all around. Everyone knows that you can bring a gun to a gunfight, but you can't just bring a gun to a Just fight. Around the bar, rumors proliferate.

"I hear they keep gunpowder in their pockets so that they'll explode when too many of them converge in one space."

"To keep them from being held as prisoners. As a tactic it's brilliant."

"I hear they don't even carry guns. They have rocket launchers."

"They give rocket launchers to toddlers!"

"They drive around in tanks!"

"They give tanks to five-year-olds."

"Those are rumors, you drunks," Xavier scoffs, but he looks worried. Reeve snaps the lighter shut and goes back to flexing his jaw.

Someone shouts, "Nick Somner's a dead man!"

"We'd be dead men, too!"

"So what do we do? He's our guy! What other use is a political party if we don't support our candidate?"

"Well, there's good drinkin' to be had!"

"Yeah, and nothing to celebrate if we're just a bunch of cowards."

Reeve has had enough. He punches Xavier in the arm, shouts, "Let's just GO," flicks out his .38 six-shooter, checks that it's loaded, and bursts out of the bar towards his motorcycle. He kicks it to life and takes off, heading south. Alone.

Back in the bar, Xavier weighs his options. He could stay with the drunken riffraff of his noncommittal comrades. Even the dapper young gentleman (known to Xavier as "Fishface," to others as "Ryan"), who had been drumming up support for a good ol' fashioned rescue and escort mission, is now on ground level with everybody else, ordering another beer and confirming the notion that heading for Utah is suicide. Xavier gives them all the finger and loads up into his truck. He catches up with Reeve two miles south.

Xavier is impressed with Reeve's emboldened act of nobility. What Xavier doesn't know is that Reeve had barely made the decision at all. He just needed to get out of there and thought he'd make a show of it. If you ask Reeve, he'll tell you that he couldn't even remember saying the words. It is only when Xavier joins him at a stoplight that he actually cements the decision to drive into Just territory.

Teamwork is funny like that.

A Friend in Need

Riley is pretty plum tuckered out and parched to boot. She's been thumbing for a ride for hours, heading west and can't find anyone to give her a seat. Come to think of it, Riley hasn't seen a car in almost two hours. The reason of course, is that she's nearly hit the West Fence, the westernmost border of what remains of the United States. It's not that she forgot about this, she merely miscalculated where the wall starts. She hadn't really seen it before. No one she knows has.

And then, just over the horizon, the great wall rises 60 feet into the sky. Huge, sheer, slate walls between giant concrete pillars. Electrified razor wire along the top. *Overkill*, thinks Riley. *Who'd want to get out to the nuclear wasteland THAT badly?* There are no gates to the outside as far as Riley can see and no guards. She tries to figure out where she is, exactly. She knows she *was* heading west from Boise and then more or less west until they hit Cannibaltown. Which puts her some 200 miles southeast of Portland, or what used to be Portland. So if she follows the wall north, she'll hit somewheres in Washington and can therefor meet up with the Scum, as per her and Clay's original plan. Riley considers this for a moment. *On second thought*, she thinks, *Seeing as how Clay is hillbilly stew right now, I think I'd rather not go hang out with those animals in Spokane. They have more drugs than brains. Or food.* Harsh thoughts, Riley, but fair. *I think I'd rather try my luck in California, supposing there's still a clan of Dissent down there. Possibly some nice Haven people.* Riley smiles. *Haven people have food that isn't people.* The smile deepens. *And showers.*

Riley makes her way south along the fence, playfully striking the fence with one of her dogchains and, inspired by the muse goddess Euterpe, begins singing a little improvisational tune. It goes something like:

I haven't eaten in days, I'm starving, I'm starving
My brain is eating itself, so hungry, I'm starving…

A noise from the road catches her attention but she doesn't see anything suspicious.

I can't eat chains, I can't eat jeans, I'm starving
Fence is not food, not food, not fair, I'm starving

She hears the noise again. It sounds to Riley's ear like

the desperate squeal of a human baby, only aged approximately 30 years and horribly dehydrated. Riley puts her back to the wall, crouches and scans the horizon for the source. She hears the noise again. Well, almost the same noise. This time it sounds like a ghost stuck in a rusty carburetor. Riley snaps the location. It's the thistle 50 yards away.

Riley sits and observes. The bush doesn't appear to be dangerous so much as it occasionally groans. Riley counts to 200 to make sure. She begins to approach the shrub slowly, twirling a length of chain. She thinks, *things that groan are generally food-based creatures.*

One track mind, that girl.

However, the closer Riley comes to the source of the noise, the less it resembles an animal that she could feast upon. The first giveaway is the clothes. *Food doesn't wear clothes.* She recalls the horrific farm that she had escaped from. *MY food doesn't wear clothes.* She gets closer still and tries to be optimistic. *Maybe someone discarded some pants and a shirt and a rabbit or something burrowed underneath and made itself a nest.* But the thing groans again and this time Riley is able to see that it was emitted from a mouth on a face belonging to a very live human head attached to a clothed body. *Shit.*

Yeah, it's just some dope dressed in a collared white shirt and slacks laying on his back in the meager shade of a juniper bush. Riley nears the man slowly, with her length of chain ready to crack down on him like a whip.

She says, "Hey!"

The person rustles and looks at her, adjusting his gaze in the sun.

"'Sup?" he manages through a dry throat.

"Are you okay?" she asks.

The man leans up and holds his head. He says, "I am *so* hungover."

He looks it, too, thinks Riley, unsympathetic. She says, "You have any money? Any food?"

The man answers this with a question of his own: "Where are the others?"

Riley scans around her and finds no trace of another human being. She asks, "What others?"

"Joey and Mack. Did they leave me here?"

Riley sighs. "Looks like it. Some friends, huh?"

"You look like you got ditched, too."

"No, but some hillbillies ate my boyfriend."

The man's eyes bug out of his head. He coughs and starts laughing.

"That's funny," he says, weakly. "How do I get back to the hotel?"

This baffles Riley. "What hotel," she asks.

"The hotel where the bachelor party was. In Frisco."

"Frisco?"

"San Francisco."

A silence falls like a blanket on the conversation, snuffing it out. Finally, Riley spits, "What the hell is San Francisco?"

Safety First

Drugs are bad, kids. Sure, ole Clyde O'Brien likes his Tennessee sour mash, his cigarettes, and the occasional doobie, but everyone knows that drugs'll mess with your brain and send you to the moon and beyond for the simple price of knowing the right dude and a crisp Hamilton. And that's bad. The Scum didn't get the memo. Other memos they did not receive: don't consume alcohol and drive, don't consume drugs and drive, and most importantly, don't consume alcohol *and* drugs *while* driving.

Or at the very least, pay attention to the road while doing so.

Clay lapses in his duty to remind the Scum of these simple memos and grips the car door handle like a runaway dog's leash. He wishes he had more buckles. He's witnessed Cody and Carly inhale about a pint of nitrous each and four beers apiece. He waves away their offers.

"No thank you! Never while I'm mobile!" he says. This is a new rule that Clay has just made up on the spot. He's never had to enforce it before. Truth be told, he could really use a beer right now but a lonely splinter of rational thought sticks in his brain— if the car goes all wreckety-wreck and Cody and Carly become tomato paste, then he'd be the one who has to drive and he's never been great at handling vehicles with a buzz on.

And really, no one is. Okay, sermon over.

Carly cracks a canister of nitrous oxide and inflates a balloon. She inhales half of the gas and holds the balloon up to Cody's lips so that he can inhale the rest. If you are thinking that this completely blinds Cody to the road ahead of him, you are correct. The same thing goes through Clay's mind and he mentions something about it.

"Don't worry about it," yells Cody over the wind, a few decibels below his usual voice. He was driving at, oh, 85 mph easily. "I got good lungs and can suck out the gas real quick. Only takes but a second and POW, I've got the whole road in my view again."

Clay is not convinced and grips the door handle tighter. It's an hour to go until Spokane. Clay considers prayer as an option. The highway convert's spiritual life is short-lived but always very devout. Clay has never prayed before and doesn't know how to start. When Cody's lead foot brings the car up to 95 mph, Clay just mutters *Oh God, Oh God* over and over again while keeping a steadfast eye open to the road ahead, sure to call out any obstruction up ahead. He has to yell a couple of times:

"COW!"

"TRACTOR!"

"OLD MAN WALKING HIS DOG—PHEW!"

Cody isn't even phased, as if nearly cleaving an old man with his hatchback is as boring as discussing oatmeal or watching golf. It could be that Cody is preoccupied with other things. He is, despite being completely twisted and hammered.

"Wait 'til we get to Spokane, man," he says in a sleazy, fake surfer dialect. Cody has never once surfed. No one Cody knows has ever surfed. No one's ever seen the ocean and as far as they know, it's become a boiling, nuclear soup of death, salt and awful stench. Kind of like Salt Lake City

"What's in Spokane? More beer?"

"And whiskey!" chimes Carly. She hasn't spoken much this entire time. Mostly she just spaces out and smiles at some things, snarls at others. This is fine with Clay, who gets nervous around girls. And since he is single as of this morning, that means every female he comes across from now on is girlfriend material. Which naturally scares the ever-living shit out of Clay (and to be honest, most of the women he could potentially talk to). Carly's voice has a particular warmth to it (behind the huskiness of a bad smoking habit) that looses a few butterflies in Clay's stomach.

Cody smiles and puts a hand on Carly's knee. Clay slackens in disappointment. It's a little bit of a relief to Clay, but the respite doesn't last long. He remembers that Cody is currently driving like a suicidal bumblebee.

Cody says, "Well, yeah, there's beer there, man! But we got something better than beer, man! Something bigger! Something that'll blow your mind!"

"What, you got a presidential candidate? A nominee? I heard the machine was going to vote today."

"Better."

"Better than a president."

"Bigger than a president," says Carly.

Clay is confused but curious. And scared. And a little bit in love with Carly.

It's a weird drive to Spokane.

All's Fair in Money and War

Salt Lake City is a fortress. After San Francisco got blown up in 1975 and the coast was walled off, venture capitalists within the fence migrated to where the money was: Salt Lake City, soon to be home of the tech boom in the New States of America. Once the political parties fissured and began militarizing, the tech companies followed. The Just is the marriage of capitalistic savvy and religious fervor, spiced with remorseless brutality. They've had two presidents serve complete terms in office. That's pretty damn efficient. They're an army on retainer— for whichever tech company offers the highest pay. Right now the Just serve the interests of Lyla Transistors.

Reeve and Xavier park just outside of the city limits, ditching their vehicles behind an empty grocery store before they hike downtown, through the alleys, until they can scope out the scene from behind a dumpster.

The Just have the city on complete lockdown. Jeeps roll through the streets as squads of well-dressed soldiers stand at attention across every block. Their uniforms are well pressed, bright yellow jumpsuits. Each soldier wears a black knit skull cap (or balaclava) and big aviator glasses. They are carrying assault rifles and side arms.

Reeve and Xavier are dressed in their shabby blue jackets and brown pants. They are carrying two pistols and a single set of brass knuckles between them. Xavier pulls up his belt and straightens his pants. Reeve slicks back his hair. They are feeling, how shall we say, a little unprepared. And self-conscious.

"I don't see any tanks," says Xavier.

"Or rocket launchers," adds Reeve.

"Amateurs," says Xavier, feigning confidence. Reeve rolls his eyes and checks his pistol. Four cartridges. Not even a full six. Reeve is beginning to think that storming out of the bar full of bravado into enemy territory was a mistake.

"Looks like this is going to take some clandestine finesse," Reeve says, also affecting confidence. Xavier nods and crouches. He puts his index finger to his mouth and shushes very loudly. It attracts the attention of the nearest Just soldier who comes to investigate. The soldier finds two frontmen running down an alleyway and so *of course* he starts firing his assault rifle in their direction. And then the rest of the squad joins him.

"RUN, REEVE!" screams Xavier. "THEY'VE SPOTTED US!"

"I swear to God, Xavier, if they kill me first, I'll haunt you for the five remaining seconds of your life!"

Bullets ricochet around them like twanging guitars. Bricks explode and pavement rips apart and flecks their pant legs. Miraculously, they skid around the corner, unharmed.

Miracles are short. For above them is a man leering down from a jeep. Make it three men in a jeep. One of them has a mounted machine gun. It begins to spin, warming up for the kill.

Xavier panics and throws the brass knuckles at the gunner. It breaks his glasses in half. The gunner swears and clutches his face. Reeve and Xavier turn tail and flee down the street. The driver changes gears and bears down on them. The passenger reads an old magazine of short stories. This is just another Wednesday for him. The gunner recovers and fires up the machine gun. The noise erupts like a Tyrannosaurus struck by lightning. The road comes apart up to Reeve's heels. This creates an uneven terrain for the jeep to pass through, generally a piece of cake for a jeep, but not one toting a .50 caliber. The gunner loses control of the spray and cuts a parked car in half before, er, *unwindowing* a delicatessen.

"In here!" yells Xavier, pointing to the door of a modest church. They run in and slam the door. The pastor is sitting in a pew, having just prayed.

He takes one look at Reeve and Xavier and says "Out."

The Frontmen take his cue and barrel down the pews, up onto the stage and through a side door, down a flight of steps, through the basement which smells of weak decaf and sugarless pastries, and out a door that leads to a small parking lot. The jeep is waiting, machine gun trained on them.

"Don't shoot! It's a church!" yells Xavier and the gunner hesitates, allowing Reeve and Xavier to run across the parking lot, ducking in between cars and keeping their heads low. They brace against the tire of a pickup truck, panting.

Xavier opens his mouth to say something fiendishly stupid before glass violently rains down on them in a single sheet.

Reeve and Xavier bolt for the mailbox across the street, only to halt suddenly as six yellow jackets pop out of an alleyway. They raise their rifles.

"Whoa," says Reeve. Xavier heel-turns 180 degrees to face the jeep. The gunner with the broken nose smiles deviously.

"Hey…" says Reeve. They throw their arms up. The machine gun starts spinning.

"There's been a huge misunderstanding!" yells Reeve. No one listens.

"We've got a piece of tech!" yells Xavier.

The machine gun stops spinning. The yellow jackets in the jeep convene and whisper back and forth. They make a hand gesture to the squadron in the alley way. Nods are exchanged.

"What are they doing?" asks Xavier.

"For the moment, they are not slaughtering us like wholesale cows. Other than that, I do not know," grits Reeve. Xavier seems pleased to have bought themselves some time.

A yellow jacket from the squadron comes forward.

"Hi!" she says cheerfully.

"Hello," says Reeve. She uppercuts him clean on the chin with the butt of her rifle knocking him out cold. Xavier stiffens.

"Hi!" she says to Xavier, equally as cheerful as before.

Xavier furrows his brow and clamps his mouth shut, sucking on his tongue. The same strike on the jaw, only this time it sounds like a clap. Xavier loses the senses of time and gravity. He feels as if he is suspended in midair, floating gently to the ground, as weightless as a feather.

None of which is true, of course. He simply keels over and slams his face into the pavement. But his cheerful assailants eyes continue to light the cavern of his unconsciousness.

The Name Game

Riley is not getting along with her newfound, hungover cohort. She doesn't like the way that he talks, all full of confusing terms and places she never heard of, served on a plate of hard-edged bravado with a side of fragile masculinity. She doesn't like the way that he talks about himself, or the way that he looks at her to see if she is impressed immediately after he talks about himself.

"Yeah, I guess you could say that I make a lot of money," says her new *friend*.

"I don't remember asking you how much you make," says Riley, staring straight ahead. She grits her teeth and tries to focus on putting one foot in front of the other.

The hungover gentleman in a dress shirt and tie deflates a little at the unenthusiastic reaction to his financial boast. He remembers something and puffs back out to full tool mode.

"Hey, you don't even know my name! My name is—"

"I don't remember asking your name."

"—Denny."

Riley ignores Denny and stomps down the road, not returning the obvious courtesy. She feels faint from hunger and thirst and currently fixates on the fear that if she stops walking, she'll keel over and fade into nothing. So she keeps going. It should be noted that she didn't invite Denny along to join her. He kind of just tagged along.

"What's your name?" Denny asks.

Riley says nothing.

Denny says, "Mary."

Riley says nothing.

"Claudette."

Riley says nothing.

"Jenny. Rose. Rachael. Kathryn. Kimberly."

Riley says nothing.

"Margaret. Faith. Chelsea. Maude. Nancy. Andrea. Victoria. Kelly."

Riley says nothing.

"Anne. Belle. Annabelle. Natalie. Caitlin with a C. Kaitlyn with a K. Angelina but your friends call you Angie. Lola. Jeanette. Amber. Theresa. Sta—"

"Jesus Christ!" yells Riley, slapping the ever-loving devil out of Denny. "It's Riley, OK? My name is Riley, you goddamn creep. Now shut up and keep walking, or shut up and stay here and die, but you *have* to shut up."

Denny shrinks, and holds his hands up in compliant

resignation. He stays a few yards behind Riley, walking in her shadow, afraid to upset her again. Until he forgets and opens his big dumb mouth.

"Hey, Riley."

"I have a headache. *Please*, just don't say anything."

"Right."

They plod along silently. The air feels like there's an electricity to it, and Riley wonders if that's because of the power lines along the highway, or the impending heatstroke. She thinks, *at least I'll*—

"Hey, Riley," says Denny interrupting her thought. "Where are we headed?"

"I don't know, dumbass. I'm just trying to get to the next town."

"Okay," says Denny. Riley hears him whistle behind her. "Hey, Riley."

"What."

"How long until we get there?"

"I don't know."

"We've been walking for miles and I'm pretty thirsty. I drank like 30 beers last night." He checks to see if this impresses her. Swing and a miss. "Do you have any water?"

"No. I do not," says Riley. She cannot tell whether her forehead is hot from fever or anger.

"Hey, Riley."

"What."

"What are your chains for?"

Riley rounds to face Denny who stops in his tracks.

She looses one of her lengths of chain and with a flick of the wrist, wraps it around Denny's neck. Denny's eyes go wide and he chuckles nervously. Riley steps on the chain, bringing Denny to his knees. She tightens the slack and moves behind Denny, putting a boot in between his shoulder blades.

"Aghkbuth!" says Denny.

Riley says, "This is what my chains are for. It's for killing poor, dumb bastards who don't keep their mouths shut."

"Okrrrgh. Gubbuadanoth," says Denny, half-choking on saliva, half-choking on his pinched trachea. She lets him go and wraps the chain around her waist again.

Denny loves oxygen. It has never really occurred to him until now that he really, really appreciates breathing oxygen. He rubs his neck and allows for a fifteen foot buffer between him and Riley before he begins walking again.

For the next few miles whenever Denny opens his mouth, Riley stops in her tracks and throws him a piercing stare and puts a hand on her chain whip.

She does this 13 times because Denny doesn't learn lessons.

The afternoon drags on, and so do our ill-matched traveling companions. They move silently, a relief for Riley's sake, but there is one caveat: when the triple threat of heat exhaustion, dehydration, and hunger looms over our heroes (compounded in Denny's case due to his monster hangover), can they tell the difference between hallucination and reality?

Riley thinks she sees a shadow pass over head. When she looks at the sky, she sees a bird pass overhead. *Goddamn vultures*, she thinks. *Can't they see we aren't dead yet?*

Worse yet is the sound of cicadas, the droning hum of insects unseen. The accumulated hiss of the insectoid mating call grows louder in her ears as a vulture circles overhead. She's caught in the bird's forceful display of power upon its landing. Unearthed dust strikes her wincing eyes— and her nose and mouth don't attempt a breath during the assault of granular soil. For a moment, primal instincts override Riley's rationality. She sees the bird and she thinks, *I can eat this.*

Tiny men depart from the vulture. She can tell that they are armed with submachine guns. Her rationality in tailspin, she thinks, *How cute. I'll stomp on them on the way to that juicy bird.* And then they get closer. Her perspective calibrates. These are soldiers—and not the two-bit soldiers of a political party, these are armed, trained, possibly military soldiers. *Full grown and unstompable foes.* It hits her. *Servicemen.*

Riley drops to the ground and her ego won't tell her whether it's because she's blinded by the dust or because she's succumbed to the superior strength of an outside force. Denny just kind of *hee-haws* like a rubbernecking yokel, not understanding the gravity of the little red dots collecting on his sternum.

Four of the tactical squad move past Riley lying in the

dirt, while two remain to check her vitals. The four move up to Denny, who is too far gone from exposure to realize the danger. It is Riley's honest belief that he thinks he's made new friends and that they are there to benefit from his charisma.

"Hey, dudes. I ever tell you guys about the time that me and Joey stole a case of beer out of a convenience store?"

A soldier forcefully ducks Denny's head down and feels his neck, while another checks his ribcage and then legs.

"No external wounds," reports one to the other.

"Nix on external head trauma."

One inspects his eyes and tongue. "GKTHB," says Denny.

"Signs of dehydration. We'll hook him up to the drip once he's in the bird."

One of the squad members by Riley jerks a thumb at her. "What about this weird chain girl?"

"You kiddin' me? Light her up."

"Okie-doke," says the soldier, taking out his side arm. He chambers a bullet and Riley's face contorts into an empty sob as she goes over her options:

1. Reach for her chains and get shot.
2. Try and run and get shot.
3. Bargain for life and get shot.
4. Get shot.
5. Shoot mouth, get shot.

"I hope you pigs fry in hell," she says. So, number 5.

"Babe," says the soldier, "We'll be gone before we even get a tan."

The joke doesn't register with Riley.

The Serviceman puts the pistol up to her head and Riley uses the last of her energy to keep her eyes open, despite the horrible, explosive noise.

Numb Skull

Clay is right to beware the dangers of driving intoxicated. He sits in the back, keeping a white-knuckle grip on his seat as Cody rockets up the highway. But just as on every other road trip ever taken in America, the mixtape in the deck starts to get old and no one packed any other cassettes. The driver, even on nitrous oxide, is sick of it and he ejects the tape and throws it out the window, to the loud protest of Carly. Middle fingers are exchanged and the only sound to guide the mood of the car is the wind and the thrumming of the tires along the pavement. Annoyed, Carly turns to sleep against the window. Bored and now less agitated by the grating music, Clay also lets his eyes fall. Without anyone to argue with, Cody, several beers and dozens of canisters of laughing gas in, also succumbs to the sweet, fried oblivion of sleep.

The hatchback plows through a motorcyclist (don't you worry, it's not our buddy, Reeve!), skids across the gravel on the shoulder and comes to an abrupt stop into a rusted speed limit sign (65 MPH, 60 TRUCKS). The sign twists and falls, cleaving through the windshield like a fish returning to water and axes poor, wasted Cody in the face.

Carly and Clay are most certainly awake now. Carly has a nasty cut on her forehead where she slammed into the dashboard and a few bruised ribs where she hit the glovebox. Clay is pretty much completely unharmed other than some whiplash and a minor abrasion on his neck from his seatbelt. Carly manages to kick open her door and she spills to the ground, lying on her back. She lights a cigarette. Clay gets out to survey the damage.

He takes one look at Cody and nearly vomits. He isn't able to see the '6'.

"He dead?" asks Carly from the ground.

"For his sake, I hope so," says Clay, retching again.

Carly asks, "The car look like it still works?"

Clay says, "I don't… I'm not good with cars."

Carly says nothing until she's finished with her cigarette, which she smokes to the filter and spits out of her mouth. She groans as she gets on her feet, checks out her totally sweet head wound in the passenger side mirror and then assesses the situation with Clay.

"We're going to have to get the sign out of the windshield," she says, perhaps overstating the obvious. She inspects her previously alive boyfriend. "…and get it out of his skull."

Together they try to yank the sign free. Cody's body follows and his head gets stuck in the windshield glass.

"Huh," says Carly. "It's really in there. Maybe if you were to try and kick out the windshield from the inside while I pull on the sign?"

Clay isn't ecstatic about this idea but, logistically speaking, it seems to be the most effective. So he gets inside the passenger seat, puts his butt up on the dash and pushes with all of his leg's strength against the windshield while Carly pulls on the twisted steel post. The windshield's structural integrity having already been compromised, however, Clay only succeeds in slicing open his ankle.

Carly gives up, lets out a sedated sigh and reaches through the driver side window and pops the trunk. She rounds to the rear of the car, rummaging for something while Clay attempts to free his bloodied leg. He untangles himself and examines his foot. Carly reappears at the front of the vehicle with a tire iron in one hand and and a fresh 16 ouncer in the other. She doesn't even wait until Clay's out of the car before she starts whipping glass. Clay tumbles out of the door, surprised. The wrath of Carly rains glass down over the dashboard and both front seats. Cody's head (and the adjoined sign) come loose and then Carly gets going on the rest of the windshield. Once it's reduced to a million cubed shards, Clay helps Carly drag Cody across the hood and they leave him stuck to the post in the gravel.

Carly casually wipes glass from the driver's seat, sits down and pops the tab from her beer.

Clay says, "Shouldn't we bury him? Like, give him a funeral or something?"

Carly nods, gets out of the car, brings the beer to her lips and spits out an ounce onto Cody's poor, abused corpse. She winks.

"That's a Scum funeral. Let's go."

Carly gets behind the wheel. Clay grabs a beer from the trunk and sits down in the passenger seat.

He thinks, *I used to have better friends.*

Taken to the Cleaners

Reeve wakes up with a dull headache behind his eyes and the feeling like he's carrying a thousand-pound ghost inside his body. Xavier is already awake and looks just about as much the worse for wear. They are on a cold, linoleum floor. There's a boring-looking man on a couch, studying both of them. He's dressed like a geology professor.

"Can I get you an aspirin? Some water?" he asks.

"Both, please," says Reeve, unaware whether he was shaking off a hangover or blunt head trauma.

"Two of each for me," says Xavier.

The boring man scuttles off to a cupboard and then to the sink and then another cupboard. Reeve takes a look around the room. He had been expecting a prison cell. Instead, he sees a laundry room turned dormitory. It smells strongly of detergent. Reeve doesn't hate it.

There's a sense of making order out of chaos here. There's also a large portion of linoleum missing from the floor, exposing cold, orangish concrete.

The man delivers the waters and medicine tablets. Xavier drinks his first entire glass of water as if it were a shot. He takes his time with his second, enjoying it like an expensive Scotch and chewing the aspirin. Reeve swishes his water around his mouth and spits it out pink. He then swallows the aspirin and chases it with the remaining liquid. He blinks a couple of times, regarding the third man with half-focused eyes.

"Thanks," says Reeve.

"You're welcome," says the man.

"Thank—," says Xavier, who chokes on a mouthful of water, coughing until his mouth is dry. "—you."

"You're welcome, too. I expect you know where we are?"

The Frontmen shake their heads.

"Oh. We're in the basement of an old apartment building. Lyla Transistors apparently bought it to house a new office branch. That's what they told me, at least."

"You get caught, too?"

The man's face falls. "You don't recognize me?"

"Nope," says Xavier. "Should we?"

"I'm Nicholas Somner," the man says. "They told me that you were sent here to rescue me."

"Oh," says Reeve, a little embarrassed at the fact that he had no idea what the current President of the New States actually looked like.

"Yeah, we're here to rescue you. We volunteered, though. We, uh, we didn't think to grab a photograph of you, or anything.'"

"Oh," says Somner. "Well, that's a little disheartening."

"But we came," says Xavier. "So that's something."

Somner laughs. "Yes. I suppose it is. Can I get you guys something to eat? There's a mini fridge in here with some decent sandwiches."

"I need a moment," says Reeve

"I'll take two sandwiches," says Xavier.

Reeve asks, "Why are you...you know..."

"Not dead?" calls Somner from the fridge.

"Yeah. The Just got to you. They aren't really known for taking prisoners."

"I'm not really sure, frankly. But they've been quite generous, as far as kidnappers go. Plenty to eat and books to read." Somner returns from the kitchenette with three sandwiches wrapped in cellophane. He hands two to Xavier. "But I suppose I can ask you the same question, yes? How come you two are still alive?" He hands a sandwich to Reeve who accepts it reflexively.

"We told them that we had info on some new tech," says Xavier, holding half a sandwich. Somner sits. Reeve puts his sandwich down and looks at it without hunger.

"It's possible that they believed you, but I'm afraid that's highly unlikely. Lyla Transistors' business model isn't focused on fair deals. They're more like pirates."

"In that they bury treasure?" Xavier asks with his mouth full.

"In that they take the treasure and bury *you.*"

Reeve says, "And yet here we are."

"And here I am," chuckles Somner. "Loyal member of the Frontmen and President of the New States and still breathing."

"I don't get it," says Reeve.

"I don't either," says Somner. "But I'm glad to have some company."

Reeve unwraps his sandwich and takes a half-hearted bite. Turkey and swiss. A stale combination. Somner leans back on the couch and stares at the light bulb in the ceiling.

"You don't have any intel on new tech, do you?"

"Nope," says Xavier, polishing off his second sandwich.

"Then maybe you're still alive because you haven't given Lyla what they need yet."

"And you," says Reeve. "You're still alive because they still have some purpose for you."

"That's just about the size of it," says Somner in a tone attempting to be jovial. "It's the *anticipation* of the whole thing that really gets to you, isn't it?" He shudders softly.

"Like terrible Christmas," says Xavier.

"Yes…" agrees Somner slowly, "like that."

Reeve doesn't say anything. He takes another bite of his sandwich and wraps it back up. Somner folds his hands on his stomach. He smiles wryly but also remains quiet.

Xavier finds a deck of cards under the sofa.

In his infinitely simple wisdom, he asks, "Anyone

remember how to play baccarat?"

There aren't any windows in the room, so it's hard for them to gauge the passage of time. They only know that it passes slowly. Nobody remembers the rules to baccarat. They play poker, but nobody really understands the rules to that game either and settle on blackjack. Somner wins five games, Xavier six, Reeve three. They eat sandwiches: egg salad, tuna salad and ham with cheddar, turkey with swiss. They make coffee and then they make more coffee. No one wants to go back to sleep. They talk about their lives, holding in the bigger revelations. Interesting things about Nicholas Somner: he's divorced, has no kids, and taught geology and math in a high school 30 years ago. After that, he helped pave roads until the day he was nabbed. Before he moved to SLC, he was a loyal member of the Frontmen and donated 50 bucks a month of his meager paycheck to their cause. He liked their devotion to blue-collar workers. His father worked on a dock in San Francisco. He drones on and on. Xavier shares that he likes beer and pinball and has a cat. He muses that it hasn't been fed since the previous morning. He's anxious for a moment, but remembers aloud that cats hunt. Reeve shares very little at all and mostly just rubs his mouth habitually.

When the Yellow Jackets finally burst through the door, it comes as some relief.

"Finally," says Reeve. "I was getting worried you forgot about us."

"Up and off your asses, gentlemen. We're going for a ride," says a feminine voice. Xavier recognizes that it belongs to the very same soldier who cleaned his clock with the butt of her rifle. He offers her a sandwich.

"Hungry?" asks Xavier. Winking. The soldier slaps the sandwich out of his hands and grabs him by the collar, ushering him out the door behind Somner and Reeve. Xavier feels the barrel of a pistol squeeze between his ribs. He also smells her pheromonal scent.

"You smell nice," he says.

"March, creep."

Led by two Yellow Jackets, with Xavier's girlfriend heading up the caboose, the prisoners are chaperoned down a hall, up a flight of stairs, out a door, down an alley and into a limousine. Xavier reaches for a bottle of brandy only to have his hand slapped away.

"Where are we going?" asks Reeve.

"Shut up," says a soldier.

"Can I have a brandy?" asks Xavier.

"No," says the soldier.

"Can *I* have a brandy?" asks Somner.

The soldier holds a breath in, trying to decide. Another soldier nods. Somner pours a tumbler full and hands it to Xavier. Reeve looks out the tinted window, watching people shuffle down the street, dodging the Yellow Jacket squads without hardly noticing them.

The limousine pulls into a basement parking structure and parks next to an elevator. The prisoners are marched into the elevator car. Xavier's gal inserts a key into the panel, turns it, and presses the button to the top floor. An extended, anxious silence is shared between the six breathing, sweating bodies.

Xavier tries to hold his breath the entire time. He comes really close to making it.

The bell dings and they file out, again led by the two Yellow Jackets and one at the rear.

The office spans the entire floor and the walls are 90% window. Reeve, Xavier and Somner have to shield their eyes against the glare. A man in a yellow suit and yellow tie sits at a desk placed precisely in the center of the room, hammering furiously into a typewriter. He doesn't acknowledge the group of soldiers and prisoners in front of him. Reeve wonders if that's a bit of a power play and rests his hands in his back pockets. The Jackets wait patiently for him to finish. Somner maintains a neutral grin with his hands clasped in front and bounces on his heels. Xavier burps brandy vapor.

The yellow-clad man finishes typing and appraises his visitors with raised eyebrows.

"Are we interrupting anything, Mr. Fulter?" asks a Jacket.

"Not at all. Just finishing some business." He gestures to Reeve and Xavier. "These are the hooligans who infiltrated the city and evaded your grasp for so long?"

Xavier's gal says, "We did catch them, sir."

Fulter says, "Yes, and only after the decimation of some local businesses. I thought I hired sharpshooters."

"You did, sir," she says. "You also hired an army. An

army devoted to neutralizing an alien threat no matter the cost."

"I did," says Fulter. "I did. You may leave now. Leave the prisoners with me."

"But, sir—"

"They're harmless. Isn't that right, boys?"

Reeve and Xavier nod excessively. Somner merely nods. The Yellow Jackets do as they are told and board the elevator. Xavier's heart breaks watching his *girlfriend* leave. Fulter waits until they are gone to light a cigarette. He spins towards the window behind him, blowing smoke at the glass.

"Somner," he says. "You know who I am?"

Somner says, "You're the CEO of Lyla Transistors, of course."

"That I am. Do you know why I haven't killed you?"

Somner groans. "I know why you would want to kill me, sir. I'm the President Elect of the New States of America."

Fulter spins around to his desk. He says, "Exactly," and reaches into his desk. Breath is bated. Fulter pulls out a remote control to a television. He clicks a button and a nine-foot-tall monolith reveals itself from behind a curtain. Another click and a prime-time show comes into grainy view. It's about a family down on their luck, but by George, do they love each other.

"Well, where's the remote, Ted?" asks the woman onscreen.

"Maybe I sold it." *Laugh track* *"...to help pay for your*

shoe addiction," says the man onscreen.

"Oh, Ted. You're always like this."

"What? Reasonable."

Applause break

"You see this?" asks Fulter. "Do you see what they've reduced us to?"

"I don't get it," says Xavier. He hiccups. "It's some dumb show."

"What does this have to do with anything?" asks Reeve, justifiably annoyed.

Somner says, "Well, it's obviously poorly—"

Fulter draws a six-shooter pistol from his desk and shoots Nicholas Somner in the sternum. Somner teeters forward and then, in correcting himself, teeters back to fall on the ground. Reeve and Xavier rush to help their comrade. Somner's dead and, unfortunately, he has no other last words.

"What the *HELL?!*" demands Reeve.

"Shh," says Fulter and waves the gun dismissively towards the television screen.

The sitcom disappears and is replaced with a bulletin:

President Elect Nicholas Somner Assassinated
Next election to be held tomorrow
Stay tuned for more developments

Fulter switches off the television and gets up to make himself a drink. He pours four glasses of bourbon into glasses and hands one to Reeve, one to Xavier, places one next to the body of Nicholas Somner, and after that, takes a drink from the glass that he gave to himself. Xavier downs his drink in one shot and stares at the floor, quietly. Fulter sits back in his chair and leisurely sips at his glass. Reeve throws his against a window. The whiskey glass shatters on impact and everyone watches as legs of liquor run down the pane. Fulter lets the moment sink in with another sip of his own drink.

He says, finally, "It's hard to understand why you're mad. Before you met him, you already presumed he was dead. Hell, we were going to kill him on sight until I had a better idea. He was a dead man the second his name was called to serve our country. The least I could do was do him myself. It's an honor thing."

"Screw your honor," says Reeve.

Fulter exchanges an icy stare. "We were going to kill *you* as well. Again, I had a better idea."

"What's that?" Reeve scoffs. "Kill us while we're taking a shit?"

"An amusing thought, but no. You two probably knew that Somner was a dead man and you came barreling into my city, anyway. That shows me that you're loyal." Fulter kicks his feet up on his desk and lets out a sigh for the effort. "Which doesn't do me any good. But it also shows that you're stupid and impulsive. In other words, it shows bravery in the face of an impossible task."

"So what?" asks Reeve.

"So, it just so happens that I have an impossible task that could use some impulsive, stupid men to attend to."

"And you can't use your Yellow Jackets, because…"

"Because the Just trust me. I need them to trust me. I need their loyalty. You can understand that. Asking them to do this would shake their faith in me. I've been working on this little project for a while now, but it's doubtful it'll succeed. The Just would think I don't have their best interests at heart. But you? Your loyalty isn't to me. I don't need it and you can keep it."

"Doesn't really incentivize us to do anything for you, as far as I can see."

"No, that's true. But if you want motivation, how about this? I can kill you now, or I can let you guys loose on a little assignment. And then you can live."

Reeve stares at Fulter with the beady eyes of an enraged wolverine. Xavier is swaying back and forth and trying really hard to keep a burp in.

"What's to keep us from turning tail and running back home?"

"I'm glad you asked that," Fulter says, hands folded in front of him. He looks giddy. He opens a desk drawer and rummages through some papers for a moment until he finds it: another little remote control with two switches. He points it at Xavier and flips one switch.

"Come on, man. Is that supposed to scare us?"

Fulter smiles and flips the other switch. Xavier falls to his knees, clutching his chest. He can't breathe and his eyes are bigger than they should be. His blood feels like concrete. Fulter switches off the remote. Xavier pants, sucking in all the air that can fit into his lungs at once.

He's pissed himself.

"It might surprise you to know that every citizen of this fine country has a little monitor attached to their heart. That monitor sends out a frequency, a signal that you're still alive. The clever minds here at Lyla Transistors have figured out a way to intercept that frequency and came up with this neat little gadget. It sends the frequency back to the monitor which then overloads. Curiously, the heart flutters and stalls. You just experienced a heart attack, my boy. How do you feel?"

Xavier vomits a fistful of sandwich and alcohol onto the floor.

"Poorly," coughs Xavier.

"Marvelous. I've got your numbers, gentlemen. I'm not afraid to call them." Fulter tosses the remote on his desk and reaches for his whiskey.

"Now," he says cheerfully. "Let's talk about my little assignment."

SCUM HAUS

The decrepit house in Spokane, Washington is rather large but still seems ill-equipped to handle all of the beater cars jammed in the driveway, all of the bodies milling around the outside porch—bodies drinking, snorting, puking, laughing, yelling and fighting—all of the pitbulls running around the yard, all of refuse, beer cans, pizza boxes and liquor bottles strewn everywhere… and although the house sits isolated from the main road, it doesn't seem like it could hold all of this *noise*. In fact, it doesn't. The men and women out front seem to bark at each other, there's the glittering tinkle of thrown glass bottles seemingly every couple of seconds, and there's harsh, thrumming, amplified country music coming from the bowels of the house.

It's Clay's kind of scene.

"Welcome to Scum Haus," Carly says with a

mischievous grin.

Clay pauses for a moment to let the name sink in. There's a pickup truck parked six inches away, boxing Clay's door. He crawls over to get out of the driver's seat, banging his knee on the gear stick. Carly leads him to the front porch. A mohawked Scum wearing a leather jacket pulls from a clear bottle of unmarked brown liquid and offers it to Carly as she climbs the steps.

Mohawk asks, "Where's Cody?"

Carly takes a slug of, presumably, whiskey. "I traded him in. This is…" She passes the bottle to Clay.

Clay takes a belt of the stuff. "I'm Clay. Formerly of the Dissent." He extends a hand and Mohawk bites it. Clay pulls it back and laughs nervously.

Everyone laughs. Clay takes a draught of the whiskey stuff.

"This is Patrick," Carly explains. "He's a worthless jackass."

"Big words for a little bitch," says Patrick.

"Oh yeah? Oh hey!" Someone grabs Carly's attention from the other side of the porch and she disappears into the crowd as if passing through a waterfall.

Patrick smiles at Clay and puts him in a headlock. Clay aims a kick at his ankles and Patrick falls on his back, laughing.

"I like it!" he says. He hops back up to his feet and slaps Clay across the chest with the back of his hand.

"Let's get you a beer," he says.

Clay follows Patrick through the door. The music is

louder inside. Everything's louder inside. Even the people. Clay's stopped by a short green-haired woman. She smiles. Clay smiles back. She punches him in the stomach.

"I'm Alice, you idiot."

Alice goes out the door. Clay buckles and gets a good view of dozens of knees. Patrick pulls him up by the collar and slaps his cheek.

"Hey buddy, you gotta be quick on your feet in Scum Haus. Come on, the kitchen's this way."

Patrick leads him through a sea of miscreants and degenerates into the kitchen where there are more of the same. The first thing Clay looks for is a refrigerator and he doesn't find one. There is, however, stacks of canned food to the ceiling in one corner of the room and flats of beer stacked to stove height in another. Patrick takes a six pack from the pile, yanks two free and hands one to Clay. The remaining four go back on the stack.

Clay pops his tab and swishes the beer around his teeth to get the remaining musk of the liquor out of his mouth. The amplified music quickens its tempo and maintains its ear-splitting volume. Patrick swigs his beer.

"It's like this," says Patrick. "The whole world fell apart and yada yada yada. After the world ends, the rats and roaches rule the earth. Now you gotta ask yourself, are you a roach or a rat?"

Clay sips his beer pensively. "What's the difference?"

"Roaches are disgusting and they can't be killed," says Pat, wiping beer from his chin. "They're also dumb, ancient little critters. But you know what really burns me about roaches?"

"What's that?"

"They ain't got no personality."

Clay pretends to think about this. Patrick continues.

"Give me a rat, any day of the week. Social creatures, sure, same as any. But you get a rat on its own and it does just as well as it would in a crew. And you jam that rat back into society? Hell, it'll eat its own brother if it were hungry enough." Patrick slams his beer, finishing it. He crushes the can against the skull of a bystander. Patrick guffaws as the poor kid clutches his head. "And you know what happens, buddy, you know what happens when you get too many rats jammed into a small space? Their goddamn tails grow together! You know what they call that?"

"A mishap?" guesses Clay. Patrick seems to ignore the answer.

"They call it a goddamn *Rat King*! Now *that's* personality!" Patrick frees another beer and lights a cigarette. He speaks from the corner of his mouth like a practiced ventriloquist. "And that's what you have here in Scum Haus," he says. "You got a buncha rats crammed in so tight that we move independently and as one. We all go out and steal food and booze and we bring it back here. I eat some of Sam's food, he eats some of mine. You see? Oh yeah, I forgot," says Patrick wiping a smirk off of his face. "You hungry?"

Clay says, "I'm... maybe later."

"Right-o. As I was saying, we got personality. We all do our own thing, but we're tied together, not by a common creed or motto— actually, we do have a motto." Patrick points at a woman with a shaved head and black lipstick. "Yo, Baldy. What's our motto?"

Baldy screams, "ONE FOR ALL AND WE'RE ALL FUCKED!"

"That's our motto. What was I saying? Oh yeah, we're tied together by depravity and necessity and all that."

Clay struggles to find Patrick's point. "So who's in charge here?"

"Buddy, you ain't listening. There ain't nobody in charge of the Scum. I know you do it differently in the Dissent. But you gotta know that kind of organization is only going to make more of the same enemy its fighting. That's the problem with organization. It organizes. The Scum? We don't have no plan, no point, no desire at all other than to spin around in circles snapping at drugs and alcohol, like a rat king. So what do you say, buddy? You want to join the Scum?"

Clay doesn't have anything else going on. "Sounds good to me, I guess."

"Awesome. What'd you say your name was?"

"Clay."

"Dumb name," Patrick grunts. He punches Clay hard in the ribs. "Your new name is Bruise. Welcome to Scum Haus, Bruise. Let me grab you another beer."

Patrick goes back to the beer stack to get the newly anointed Bruise another refreshment. Clay holds his side and slows his breathing, looking to the ceiling to gain focus.

"How you liking Scum Haus?" a familiar voice asks him. Carly appears at his side holding a bottle of vodka in one hand and some sort of inhalant in the other.

"I think I like it?" says Clay with a hint of hesitation. "Apparently my new name is Bruise." He massages his kidney.

"I doubt it'll stick. Patrick calls everybody Bruise. It gives him an excuse to punch new people. He likes to punch people when he gets drunk. Between you and me, he's got a bit of a problem." Carly breathes in a lungful of whatever godforsaken inhalant she's holding. Her pupils dilate like a kitten's.

She asks, "You catch any of the show yet?"

Clay finishes his beer and throws the can at somebody. He likes how that feels. He says, "No, I haven't."

"Well come on, dumbass!"

Carly leads Clay by the hand through the kitchen to a hallway that connects to a stairwell. Clay can't help but feel excited at the touch of Carly's sweaty little hand. They have to break the hand holding to descend the stairs but Carly is quick to reconnect when they hit the landing. Clay smiles.

The basement contains the fermented smell of ancient and recent molds mixed with the sweat of too many crowded, bouncing, liquor-filled bodies. The air is made out of noise, and Clay feels like he's walking through sludge as the amplified bass blows out another speaker.

The music is definitely rooted in country and blues but the instrumentation is sloppy and the vocals are slurred and tinged with aggression. Someone knocks into Clay. Carly knocks that person back. Elbows start flying— Clay ducks and throws his weight at three thickset Scum who catch him, spin him around and launch him back where he came from. Clay laughs when he gets to his feet. He wipes the sweat— some his, mostly not— from his brow. *The Rat King*, he thinks. *I get the Rat King. The chaos of many moving parts coalesced into one organism.*

A sideways fist knocks some of Clay's teeth loose and he tastes blood. He leaves the pit, hand to his mouth, looking for Carly. He can't see her and goes back to the stairwell door. He finds Patrick blitzed out of his mind and excited to find his new buddy Bruise once again.

"Bruise!" Patrick yells over the music. Clay nods at him and dodges the headlock. Clay scurries up the stairs and slides down the hall through cigarette and marijuana smoke and emerges again in the kitchen. There's no sink. Clay grabs a beer, pulls the tab, swishes it around in his teeth and spits pink onto the shirt of a kid with more piercings than face. Pierce laughs.

"Is there a bathroom around here?" Clay mumbles.

Pierce says, "Yeah," and points towards the foyer. "There's a door. You'll find it."

Clay passes through a tight knot of people and eventually finds a doorknob. He yanks it open and passes through. The walls are graffitied so thick, no one tag is distinguishable. A young woman holds onto the bowl of a seatless toilet, apparently in love with it. Clay checks the walls. There's no mirror.

"There's no mirror," he says, perplexed, to the porcelain lovebird.

"Why the hell would you want a mirror?" she asks. She laughs and vomits. Clay rubs his mouth. And his ribs. He leaves the young woman alone with the toilet.

Clay goes out to the front porch to sit on the stairs, feeling lonely amidst four hundred people spilling out of a house. He no longer understands the Rat King and feels no love for the concept. He asks a studded jacket for a cigarette and is pelted with a pack. Clay sits, smokes and drinks his beer, asking himself a deplorable question: does he want to go back home? The grisly image of Cody's double face finds his thoughts.

A hand appears on his shoulder.

"Bruise!" yells Patrick, sitting himself on the stoop next to Clay. "I found ya." Patrick slaps his knees and asks for a cigarette. Clay passes one and Patrick lights it and speaks softly and strongly under the uproar of Scum Haus.

"I get it," he says. "Right about now you might be regretting the choices that led yourself here. I know that game. I've been there myself a few times. You got a little roughed up and I ain't going to apologize for that, because it's rough around here. That's how we do it Scum style. But it hurts and I know that hurt and I don't want you to feel like we don't know that hurt." Patrick looks off into the long, dark driveway. "But don't run, man.

None of us here would call it weak if you did. Ain't no punishment if you do. But it ain't fun, man. It ain't fun out there, alone."

Clay and Patrick feel the toe of a boot bluntly knock them in their shoulder blades. Carly hangs over them holding a pipe.

"You louse-ridden miscreants not having a good time?" she asks.

"Bruise here is a little homesick, is all," says Patrick.

Carly sways on the stairs, using her pipe like a wand in the air to spell out her words in sweeping flourishes. "Well, we got something to bolster his spirits, don't we?"

"We do?" asks Patrick.

"We do," confirms Carly. She grabs Clay by the elbow and he gets to his feet uneasily. He's feeling a little woozy and overwhelmed by the bold choices he's recently made. Carly grabs Patrick by his elbow and yanks him to his feet as well. Patrick is feeling a little woozy by the near-lethal amount of alcohol and cousin substances that he's been imbibing since his noon-time breakfast. Clumsily, the three walk down the steps and through the lawn. The music from the basement sounds unearthly now, just a tinny reverberation. The grass wets their pant legs and a frosty chill makes plumes out of their breath but Clay's spirits are improving. Perhaps it's the alcohol or perhaps it's the safety of finding friends, *fellow rats*. Although he's had better friends, he's never made this many for simply showing up.

Carly says something and Patrick laughs and Clay

realizes that he's laughing too. He's in love with the moment of laughter, afraid to let it go. No one lets go of the laughter or each other, all the way to the shed. And then finally, when they reach the sad little shack, Carly breaks off and puts her hands on the door handle.

"Are you ready for this?" she giggles. She flings the door open.

Patrick's laughing, whether at what he sees or just out of momentum, it's hard to tell. Clay's chuckle winds down as he surveys the inside of the shed: he sees shears, a lawnmower, a couple of forgotten terracotta pots, a chainsaw, a few trowels, a metal case containing the launch codes for a thermonuclear bomb, a rake, a shovel, some garden gnomes...

Perspiration beads on Clay's confused brow. His laughter betrays his anxiety. Patrick slaps him on the back.

"Pretty cool lawn mower, huh?"

Purgatorio

The explosive noise that rings in Riley's ears is none other than Denny's blood-curdling, throaty yelp.

"WAIT!" he screams. The soldier flinches and looks at Denny, bemused and irritated.

"That's my girlfriend!" Denny pleas. The soldier sighs and deflates a little. His pistol's still aimed at Riley's temple. And her eyes nearly burst from their sockets as she literally bites her tongue. *Okay,* she thinks. *What's going to hurt less, here? A bullet in the brain, or playing along with this jackass?* She begins to hyperventilate, a side effect of the adrenaline catching up with her mixed with the possibility of life, continued. Riley clenches her eyes and opens them, readjusting to this new plan.

"It's true," she says. "I love the dope."

The soldier relaxes his aim, slightly. The gun is still pointing in Riley's direction, but it's deescalated to a maim shot. The Serviceman smiles and looks at Denny.

"Is that right? So that's why you scaled the wall, eh, buddy?"

Denny's brain gears turn slowly, all jammed up with hungover gunk. He returns the smile.

"That's it," he says. "I wanted to see her."

Riley thinks, *So he's from the other side of the wall. He... he didn't know he was on this side of the wall?*

"Well, I've been there, brother." The soldier turns to laugh with the other soldiers. "So, what's this weird girl's name?"

Riley braces for the worst.

"Miley," Denny says. *Close enough, idiot.*

"And how'd you meet Miley, here? If you've been crossing the border before, we need to know that. It's a big problem if you have."

Denny's eyes flutter as he mentally rolodexes through some lies. He lands on, "I used my dad's uplink." Denny seems satisfied with that explanation but the soldier looks horrified. Denny says, "Please don't tell him! I just thought she was pretty! I managed to get her on the phone a couple of times before and I don't know, I just wanted to meet her in person!"

The soldier buys it but Riley can tell that Denny just saved her life by falsely admitting to something dangerously stupid. The pistol is raised once again at Riley's head.

"Come on, Denny," the soldier says soberly. "She's seen you. You used his console? That means she knows about your dad. Shit. It's too close, man. She can compromise us if we let her run back to her friends. We nip these things in the bud. That's what we do."

Denny raises his hands. He is squinting in the sunlight but his face looks genuine when he says, "We can take her with us."

"You know that's not allowed."

"Well, it's gonna have to be," argues Denny.

"Or what?"

Denny stands straight and any sense of fun and dumb party boy evaporates from his demeanor. He beckons all of the dignity from the bottom of his throat to say, "Or it's your ass, Gene."

"You can't make that call," says Gene the Serviceman.

"I don't have to. I can make the call to the Deportation Office. Your wife's sister's got a hefty rap sheet and I've seen it. You want to explain to Cathy that you could've prevented her getting hauled away?"

"You wouldn't *dare*. We went to school together, man."

"I know we did. So put that gun down. Either Miley goes out..." Riley winces again at her butchered name. "...Or Cathy goes in. Your call."

It's not too late to chain-whip this bastard and hijack the helicopter for myself, thinks Riley. *But then, I've never flown in one of those...*

The Serviceman surrenders to Denny's surprisingly well argued gambit. The pistol gets holstered and Riley's hauled to her feet with a rough yank of her arm.

"You lucky little bitch," says Gene. Riley smiles.

"You can call me Miley, *Gene.* Thanks for not popping me."

Gene swears in disgust and gathers the other soldiers for extraction. Denny takes a deep breath and remembers how hungover he is. Upon his exhale, he rests his chin to his sternum and lets his shoulders sag. Riley slowly walks over to him, and carefully thinks of an appropriate thing to say.

"Thanks," she decides to say. "I know you didn't have to do that."

Denny, shading his eyes from the sun and, adopting a foolish grin, says, "Of course I did. If we have any hope to get married, that is."

Riley decides not to strangle him again. A soldier comes and aids Denny onto the chopper and another soldier comes to aid Riley as well. They get buckled in and a medic administers an IV drip to them both. Riley feels life course through her veins and the hot fog in her head clears, leaving a cool, focused feeling. Denny falls asleep before the helicopter blades are spinning. Riley remains alert and quietly agrees that getting into a helicopter with strangers is better than dying in the desert, better than getting shot point blank for apparently knowing too much. The helicopter blades reach the desired rpm and the bird takes off clumsily from the sand. Riley holds onto her seat. Gene chews a piece of gum, sneering into a smile.

"Never been in a bird before, huh? Of course not. You ain't been allowed. Well, consider this a miracle, darling."

The helicopter rises in the air and corrects its direction. Riley can see the wall below her dividing two stakes of desert. *Some miracle,* she thinks. The helicopter noses west and Riley is unable to take her eyes from the scene below: full forests and rivers and other greenery. Gene giggles.

He says, "You've never seen this kind of land before. I almost envy you. But then I remember if I were *you,* I'd just be an idiot who couldn't appreciate the scene. It'd be like wasting a sirloin steak on someone who's only ever eaten clumps of dirt." He guffaws. "If I was born an idiot, who knows? Maybe I'd prefer the dirt after all."

Riley aims a kick just behind Gene's shin guard. She kicks repeatedly until she feels his patella reverberate against her boot. Once again, there's a pistol aimed at Riley's head.

"Watch it, simpleton. I'm allowed to take defensive action. I could shoot you and throw your body from a thousand feet in the air." A cruel smile twists through Gene's lips. "Maybe I wouldn't bother shooting you and throw you anyway."

Riley takes hold of her temper. She's calm and collected. She says, "How'd you square that with your sister in-law?"

Gene frowns and bounces the weight of the gun in his hand. He's the type of guy who likes the small sound of a cartridge jangling slightly in the chamber. "Your boyfriend is asleep, darling. You can't make his threats for him."

"That doesn't change your agreement with poor, sleepy Denny, here."

"It could be worth it," he snarls. "You just give me a reason, little girl."

A soldier hits Gene softly on the shoulder. "Let her alone, man. Don't you go heaping trouble on yourself, again." Gene's face looks like he just opened a dumpster of rotting meat. But he holsters his gun and stares hard at the window.

Some time passes and Riley still refuses sleep. She doesn't trust it. She looks out the window, amazed at how the landscape continues to change. And then the air changes— the helicopter flies through crisp, salty vapor. Riley finds it refreshingly intoxicating. She can't seem to inhale enough air through her nostrils. Of course, this gives a soldier the impression that she's hyperventilating.

A soldier asks, "Are you okay?"

Riley looks perplexed. "I'm fine. I've just never smelled air like this before."

The soldier chuckles. She says, "That's the smell of the ocean. Means we're getting close."

A fist sized clump of panic sticks in Riley's throat. "The ocean?" she says. "But it's radioactive."

The soldier looks at her and chuckles again. She says to Riley, "What are you *talking* about?"

Embarrassed, Riley turns to look below. The city of San Francisco's hard edges poke out from the horizon. When it gets closer in view, Riley anticipates a hollow city of nuclear disaster, buildings standing out of sheer stubbornness against entropy. What she sees, however, is a busy and crowded metropolis situated uncomfortably around a bay and wedged into the crevices of rolling hills, undeniably thriving. Riley's eyes are saucers. She doesn't say anything, lest she invite more derision or pity from the soldiers around her.

Gene smirks. "Cat got your tongue?"

"Dog got your balls?" Riley spits.

"Your naiveté must be what Denny finds so cute. Ain't that right, pal?" Gene reaches over to slap Denny on the knee. Denny snaps awake. Riley doesn't think his eyes look right— they're fluttering around in their sockets. Foam gurgles from his mouth.

"UM!" Riley yells, pointing to her "new boyfriend."

"Oh shit," says Gene. He unbuckles his belt to check Denny's pulse. Another soldier removes a glove and sticks it in Denny's mouth.

"He's seizing!" The soldier twists into the cockpit and makes some hand gestures Riley doesn't understand. The helicopter changes course. Riley holds onto Denny's hand which is more of a claw now. Chauvinist jackass or no, the kid saved her life. The helicopter swings into San Francisco and hones towards a tall building with an encircled H on the roof. The landing is quick and the bounce makes Riley's stomach flop. Paramedics are waiting with a stretcher and they get Denny laid out in a matter of seconds. It seems to Riley that she blinked and they were gone. The Servicemen are gone too, having escorted the medics into the building. Only the pilot remains with the bird, smoking a cigarette in the cockpit.

She asks, "Do I..."

"Get out," the pilot says.

Riley removes the IV from her arm and does as she's told. She stands out on the roof alone, taking in the vista of San Francisco's lights gleaming in the dusk. The orange shimmers along a gentle tide in the bay and the Golden Gate Bridge stands like a horizontal beacon of light, cutting through the water. Riley breathes slowly, soaking this all in. After she's taken enough pause, she realizes she's not alone. She feels a Serviceman's presence on her shoulder. She feels eyes scan the dog chains around her waist and the dusted, torn clothing falling off her body. She hears the release of a breath. She knows that he knows she's not a threat. Riley feels a little disparaged.

"Riley Owen?" the Serviceman asks.

"You must be confused," Riley says. "Name's Miley. You can ask Denny when he comes to."

"Cute. You're wanted somewhere. I'll have you come with me, please."

Riley makes a face. "Pretty polite words for such a rude request."

"Yeah, well. We're trained to have some manners. Makes it easier to interact with the populace." Riley hears the sound of cloth shuffling. *He's straightening his goddamn tie.* She then hears him clear his throat. "But it wasn't a request."

Riley turns to face him. "Where am I going?"

"A certain somewhere."

"Like a certain cemetery?"

"Until I hear otherwise, you are not to be harmed."

"Just a moment," she says. She slowly rotates 360 degrees, letting the sunset wash over her. She's overwhelmed by it's beauty at first but then she breathes it in, storing the scene somewhere deep, making it a part of her. She exhales calmly.

"Okay," she says finally. "Let's go."

The man leads her into the building and they board an elevator which rockets to the bottom floor and Riley feels a nausea not unlike that of the helicopter landing. She follows the Serviceman to a sedan and they drive off through the bright streets. Riley's seen cities before, sure. But not one with 100% working electricity. She doesn't see a single bullet hole in the windows they drive past. The Serviceman twists on the radio and the sound of heavy bass and deep, rippling beats fills the car as a singer rhymes lyrically about violence and amassing wealth. Riley loves it.

They drive to an exclusive suburb where the houses are as big as small castles. The car parks in front of a modest mansion. The Serviceman opens the door for Riley and he walks her to the door and nods at the Serviceman standing post.

"Riley Owen?" the man asks. Riley's Serviceman nods again. "Go on in."

The foyer's floor is polished oak. There are family portraits on the wall as well as glossy framed photographs of a bearded man meeting with celebrities Riley's never even heard of. A banjo and a guitar hang on pegs, both marked with an illegible signature. Riley is marched through this into a living room of a few couches and a gigantic television screen. The room feels as if it's rarely ever been inhabited— Riley notices that the television is unplugged. They walk through an alcove that seems to split off to the kitchen and a staircase leading to the basement. They descend to the basement where they encounter yet another Serviceman guarding a door.

"He ready?" Riley's Serviceman asks. The other doesn't say anything but opens the door for them to walk through. Riley's gives her a nudge.

"Come on. You first."

Riley enters and her heart palpitates. The basement room is wallpapered with small, flat television screens— Riley estimates there must be about two hundred of them. Each one alternates one image after another. Riley sees footage of an open plain, followed by a familiar wall covered in snow, followed by a dark city street where people are gathering on the sidewalk, followed by an aerial view of buildings breathing fog through their smokestacks. Every single screen alternates footage every three seconds, seemingly never repeating the same image. It's kaleidoscopic.

Then, on a screen on the far wall next to a man sitting serenely in a chair she sees herself walking down the stairs of this very house, pausing for the Servicemen to let her through the door. And then she watches herself go through the door. The screen turns to footage of her walking through the door and freezing. A different screen shows her standing there, looking startled and confused. She notices it's just her alone on the screen. She spins around to find that the Serviceman that escorted her never entered the room. She turns around and warily looks to the man sitting in the chair.

I spin around in my chair and take a sip of Tennessee sour mash.

I say, "Hello, Riley Owen. I'm glad you could make it. "

I get up to shake her hand which she looks at as if its made of snakes.

I say, "You might've heard of me. I'm Clyde O'Brien, former President of the New States of America."

Riley just goes and barfs on my carpet.

Something's Amiss...

Clay wakes up with a savage hangover. His mouth tastes like it's made out of sand and his eyes are carved out of fogged glass. He's lying facedown on a pile of foul-smelling clothes and the washing machine and dryer indicate that he passed out in the laundry room last night. His eyes adjust to the machines. The dryer is burnt out from the inside—someone must have thrown in a firework at some point— and the washing machine has a big marijuana plant growing from its tub. Clay isn't alone in the room, either. An obese teenager with a septum piercing cuddles a raccoon while asleep in the corner while another pierced drunkard wakes up in the sink. She blinks at Clay and then falls back to sleep.

The house is moving, with people milling around, but it's more of a slight vibration compared with the previous night's bombastic energy. Everyone seems to be be undergoing one nutritional deficiency or another due to overindulgence. Some go back to it, cracking open beers on the porch while others light up in the living room. Clay goes to the kitchen, where he finds a man in a faded baseball cap cooking four cans of corned beef hash at once.

Baseball cap coughs and covers his mouth with a dish cloth.

He asks, "Breakfast?"

Clay accepts a plate of delicious slop. He can't find any silverware. He grabs a beer and takes his meal outside on the porch to, in his words, *eat via gravity.* More Scum gradually join him with plates of hash and no utensils. Most eat with their hands and some with their tongues. It's a strange meal shared with strange people but Clay is feeling almost happy. As the protein mush begins to rejuvenate and revitalize his body, he feels accepted. He's always been weird and now he's among people like him, his own tribe. He thought he'd found a family in the Dissent through a shared ideology. Now he realizes that he didn't need an ideology, just the family.

But there is something that frightens him. It's not the people themselves—he likes the people— but something between the people. Perhaps, something lacking.

Something missing.

Clay returns to the kitchen to clean his plate and thank the baseball cap guy for cooking. But Clay doesn't find the baseball cap guy at the stove (where a frying pan full of hash still burns on the flame). He finds baseball cap in the living room, hitting a fat doobie while eating his own meal.

"Shouldn't you be watching the food?" Clay asks.

"What?" baseball cap asks.

"The food's burning."

Baseball cap shrugs. "So unburn it."

Scratching his stubble, Clay returns to the kitchen and reduces the heat on the stove to low and stirs the hash around to spread out the exposure to heat. Scum came and went. Clay fills up their plates with corned beef hash, whether it's fully cooked or not, whether it's burnt or not. No one can find utensils, no one cares. A girl in sunglasses and a leather jacket thanks Clay. Some guy in a flannel shirt with a beard gives Clay a beer.

Says, "My compliments to the chef."

Clay opens four more cans of corned beef hash and adds them to the pan. After giving out six more plates, he decides he's bored of cooking and leaves it sizzling on the stovetop. Either someone will take his place or they won't. Clay smiles. Scum life. Rat King philosophy.

A girl in a striped dress and a fedora spray paints obscenities on the wall in cursive. A blob of leather jackets grope each other on the couch. Someone starts a fire in the fireplace and someone else throws a firecracker into it, spraying hot ash and cinders all over the living room floor. Clay helps extinguish it with his beer, laughing. A good-natured punching match ensues and Clay ducks out of it and goes up the stairs to see the rest of the house.

Each room is packed with Scum too hung-over to get out of bed. They throw bottles at the door. Clay isn't quite cognizant of why he's just kind of prowling around the grounds. If he would be honest with himself, he'd perhaps recognize that he's looking for Carly. He can't find Patrick either. If Clay, again, would be honest with himself, he'd recognize the unnerving stab of anxiety in his lungs as jealous suspicion. Clay goes outside to get some fresh air.

The Scum outside have organized a game of beer pong and Clay watches, resting his arms on the wooden rail and scratching his head. He bats away the pangs of anxiety. He recalls a snippet of conversation:

"Hahaha! They won't know what hit 'em!"

"No one'll know what's going on!"

"Brilliant. Absolutely brilliant."

But who said what? Did it matter? Clay shakes his head and looks for cigarettes to bum. He doesn't find any, but he does find a seventeen-year-old kid setting up liquor bottles on tree stumps. Clay walks by and inspects the liquor bottles and then looks to the kid, now kneeling in the grass some 20 yards away.

"You have any smokes, kid?" Clay calls to him.

A bottle explodes next to Clay. The kid's lying prone with a silver .38 in his hand.

"Jesus!" Clay yells, brushing off shards of glass from his arms, shirt and pants.

"Clear the line of fire," the kid says in a tranquil voice.

Clay edges to one side, allowing at least 60 degrees of

clearance between him and the muzzle, then sidles back towards the kid until he's standing squarely behind him and the gun.

"You almost shot me," Clay says.

"Mm," acknowledges the kid. He squeezes off another round and another bottle turns into glitter.

"Have you seen Carly?" Clay asks.

"Who?"

"What about Patrick. You know Patrick?"

"I don't. They're both equally worthless. Maybe I've met them, but I wouldn't know their names." Another gunshot and glass explosion like a call and response or some kind of twisted rhyme.

Clay scratches his head again.

"I don't smoke," the kid says. "So I wouldn't have any cigarettes. But if you want to shoot some bottles with me, there are some guns lying around."

Clay considers this. He finds the idea pretty bitchin'.

"If I wanted to find a gun," Clay asks. "Where would I find one?"

"You could check the shed," the kid says in a serene, focused voice. "That's where I found Lil Debby here." He gestures with the pistol towards the shed.

Clay lets a quick feeling of anxiety pass over him. He knows that shed. But from when? Last night?

There was something in there... something... bad?

Clay opens the shed doors. Rakes and shovels, trowels, and a lawnmower. The knot in Clay's stomach relaxes. There's a green metal box with a star on it behind some terracotta pots. Clay pulls out a snub nosed six shooter and a handful of bullets and rejoins the kid at the "shooting range."

"Best to kneel if you can," the kid says. "Helps absorb the impact. I like to lay on my stomach. It seems to help with my aim." The kid fires off three shots, two bottles killed, one dead twice.

Clay kneels beside him and presses the cartridges through the loading gate. He takes aim and—*aw shit* —removes the safety. Clay fires off three rounds, one bottle killed.

"Pretty fun, huh?" says the kid.

"Pretty fun," confirms Clay. He's shot a gun before, but doesn't want to admit it. His aim is pretty weak.

"Pretty fucked up, what we got in the shed, huh?" the kid says. *BANG.*

"What's that? A box of guns?" replies Clay. He takes a shot. *BANG.*

"Naw, man." *BANG.* "The bomb trigger by the lawnmower." *BANG.*

A familiar sensation of dread creeps up Clay's spine. He tries to shoo it away.

The kid says, "You just never know when someone's gonna get drunk enough and set the damn thing off, don't you? That's what makes this place fun."

"Yeah..." says Clay out of reflex. "No... no, there wasn't... it's not in the shed."

The kid stops shooting. "It isn't?"

Clay clears his throat. "No. It isn't."

The seventeen-year-old crack shot thinks this is the funniest thing in the entire world.

Driving Shotgun

Reeve drives. Xavier sits in the passenger seat of the jeep. Rebecca, the previously unnamed soldier who cleaned Xavier's clock, the very same woman that Xavier had supposedly fallen in love with, sits in the back seat with a shotgun resting on her lap. They munch on a meager breakfast from a gas station. Reeve chews through a stick of jerky. Xavier crunches on fried corn (pissing the hell out of Reeve). Rebecca keeps her eyes on the two Frontmen while removing a tiny, powdered donut from a roll of tiny, powdered donuts and dropping the whole thing in her mouth, letting the powdered sugar dissolve against her tongue before chewing the rest.

Reeve isn't sure if they are in Kansas, Colorado or Nebraska.

They drive.

Lunch is tinned meat, which they eat in a parking lot,

followed by a donut and a coffee each, consumed while driving. Xavier eats his donut and falls asleep without touching the coffee. Rebecca chases an oral stimulant with her coffee and shakes the silvery ghosts of amphetamine psychosis from the corners of her eyes. Reeve eats half of his donut and quaffs down his entire coffee. The radio drones on about the next election. Reeve switches it to a local channel, which is apparently under the control of the Truth Bearers. The DJ lists off a string of sinful citizens in the surrounding area codes.

Reeve hears, "Christopher DeGaulle, suspected of coveting his neighbor's wife. Andrew Kaine, suspected of local due evasion. Susanne Quimby, suspected of allowing ingress to unfavorably aligned individuals. Martine Ruiz, suspected of transporting disallowed items for purchase across Truth territory. Alicea McDowell, suspected of hoarding more than necessary foodstuffs allowed…"

Dreary words to match the landscape. Reeve switches the radio off. He looks in the rearview to see Rebecca wiping her shotgun with a rag.

"So," he says. "You're from Utah?"

"Indiana," she replies. "Initially."

"Is that right? I was born and raised in Idaho." Small talk is not in Reeve's wheelhouse. "So, you left Indiana?"

"Obviously."

"How come?"

Rebecca doesn't actually want to answer that. And usually she wouldn't. But right now, the drug in her system is giving her a choice between talk or ground molars.

"Because where we are now is Truth territory. Where I'm from is mostly run by the Forgiveness with an uneasy alliance with the Skull Mongers."

"How's that worse than the Truth Bearers? Hell, how's that worse than the Just?"

Rebecca rubs some enamel off her teeth before answering.

"The Truthers will at least broadcast their targets before closing in. Gives some folk some notice and the chance to escape. The Forgiveness just go in for the kill. And they're happy to do it. At least they think they are. They think that extracting the soul through a bullet in the head means that they're saving the poor bastard." She lets out a bitter laugh. "A bullet if you're lucky." Rebecca stares at the ocean of plains on the other side of the window. She mutters, "They believe the body is too sinful to exist." She bites her thumb nail and adds, "...if the body isn't suited for the Lord's work."

There's silence for a while. Reeve's eyes fog over and threaten to clam shut. He reaches for Xavier's untouched coffee and pulls it to his lips. The lid pops off and half the cup falls directly onto Reeve's groin.

Reeve makes a guttural noise from the bottom of his throat, as if his vocal chords were torn between swearing and screaming. The car swerves onto the gravel shoulder and fishtails. Xavier snaps awake, eyes wide. Rebecca, thinking that Reeve might be pulling a fast one, props the shotgun on Reeve's arm rest, barrel pointing at his head. Tires bite into the gravel as Reeve corrects the car and everyone takes a few breaths to calm down.

After the coffee cools and a few miles of straight road passes in the rearview, the party's mood and energy regulates. Xavier falls back asleep and Reeve drinks the rest of the coffee, a nearly redundant gesture now, as the near collision, along with the searing pain of his testicles and the threat of the back of his head being opened by buckshot, had pretty much chased away any spectre of drowsiness from his mind.

Rebecca's eyesight is still spinning. The shotgun is back in her lap and she's working on regulating her breathing. *In for one-one-thousand, two-one-thousand, three-one-thousand, four-one-thousand, five-one-thousand... out for one-one-thousand, two-one-thousand, three...*

Reeve watches her breathe in the rearview. He can hear the pronounced jingling of the grenades strapped across Rebecca's vest with every exhale. After a couple of cycles, he decides to continue their conversation.

"What about the Just?" he asks.

The question startles Rebecca out of her meditation.

"What about the Just?" she replies.

"How are they any different from the Forgiveness? The Truth Bearers?"

Rebecca scowls. "How're the Frontmen different from the Just?"

"Working class values," replies Reeve without blinking. "A dedication to the concept that every single person belonging to this nation deserves the same basic rights and opportunities to succeed and survive."

Rebecca doesn't blink either. "You can say the same about the Just."

"*You* can say the same about the Just. I can't."

"Yeah? And why not? Listen, my party believes that those opportunities are already there and we wish to secure those opportunities. Why else could companies like Lyla Transistors succeed? How could anyone? And yet people are succeeding."

"*Some* people are succeeding, and very rarely. Others are slaughtering each other in the streets for the chance to survive."

"And yet the opportunities are there. That's what this is about, right? I had no better chance of survival than you did and yet here we both are."

"You don't think something can be done? Companies like Lyla survived because pre-existing circumstances that the rest of us didn't have."

"Call it a pillar of reliability, then, and quit being so butt-hurt that your team ain't at the top."

Blood leaves Reeve's knuckles as he keeps the next few thoughts to himself. Rebecca regulates her breathing. After six more cycles, she breaks the silence.

"My guys and your guys want the same thing, I think. We want stability while navigating this new messed-up national landscape. We're desperate for it. The Truth Bearers and the Forgiveness? They want the stability of the Old Law. Pre-American religious nonsense."

"And the Just serving a Mormon enterprise? You don't find that kind of hypocritical?"

"The Just seek out the most beneficial circumstances for its soldiers. It's a part of the party's religious beliefs. We're all well-fed, have comfortable barracks and are allowed an allowance, most of which soldiers send back home to their families. We're not fanatics. We're an army with savvy business ties."

"Bullshit," Reeve mutters. "I took a look around Salt Lake City and it looked like martial law."

"People are safe and are free to live their lives as they see fit within the confines of the law as we see fit to enforce."

"That isn't living," Reeve says. He sucks the last few remaining dregs of coffee out of the cup. "What you're describing is corporate fascism. Military in the street? Protecting a company's interests? Backed by a religious congregation? Come on. Who's it serving? Answer me that, who's it serving?"

Rebecca tongues her teeth compulsively. She answers, "The common man. People are afraid. It's better to be afraid of us, who'll have a reason to kill you, instead of being afraid of your neighbor, who'll kill you for no reason at all. We're serving everybody."

"Everybody? Sounds like it's serving only the people in charge."

"Well, they're in charge. Do you want to be in charge?

"Me, personally? No. But I'd want the person that's in charge to at least have me in mind. To make sure that companies can't hire private armies to hold stake on an entire city."

"You think if the Frontmen ever got their shit together, if they could gain control over a city, that it would be any different? You'd just have different propaganda, explaining the state of things in a way that justifies you, the Frontmen. It'd be the same. At least the Just has infrastructure. A vision, and yes, I don't agree with all of it. But what do you have? A bunch of angry leftists, scattered here and there, grumbling about how the world should be while ignoring how the world really is?"

"Goddammit, we're grumbling, as you say, because the world is how it is, we *are* realistic in that perspective and we can do better. I believe that. I believe that we can, at least, make the meaningless shit, the work, the pressure and stress actually count for something. I believe that if we can take just a chunk of that burden off of those who've been put under the thumb of corporate interests, *then*, I believe we can march toward a future worth remembering."

More silence in the car, save for Xavier's snoring. Reeve keeps the vehicle at a steady 75 mph.

It appears as a dot on the horizon and then as a looming silhouette. Reeve mistakes it as a bird's nest on a telephone pole, but quickly learns better. It's a telephone pole, alright. This one's been modified into a crucifix. And so have a dozen other poles. The crucifixes stand in a line, holding the decapitated corpses of a few unlucky souls by their hands and feet.

Rebecca mutters a prayer under her breath. Reeve hears the word, "*Forgiveness.*"

Reeve white-knuckles the steering wheel and keeps his eyes tight on the road as he he accelerates to 90 mph.

Xavier snores softly.

Clyde O'Brien Time

Old Clyde O'Brien had you going for a while, didn't he? Don't be embarrassed, you're not alone. Millions of Americans in the Inner Circle bought it hook, line and sinker: I was gunned down in my house by the Just. HA! You know how they say that Washington could never tell a lie even when he was looking at a belting for chopping down his papa's cherry tree? And ole Honest Abe, who never had a single deceitful neuron in his brain? Sure you do. But Clyde O'Brien? Whoo-ee, he's full of shit.

So let me set the record straight and let me tell you what ain't horse puckey— I did indeed brave the journey that I described earlier and I did indeed serve as the New States' first president almost exactly as I described. However, I wasn't gunned down by the Just after my term ended. No, that would have been just slightly too convenient, don't you think?

But every one bought it. And it set the precedent of violent assassinations ever since. What a legacy!

No, the Servicemen loaded me up into a helicopter shortly after my time ended and they brought me first to Seattle— I imagine that they would have brought me to the East Coast, but it wasn't bullshit that D.C. was absolutely decimated. What I learned, though, was the nuclear attacks on the coasts, the reports that I was given, the reports that led to my decision to wall off the so-called Inner Cirlce, were completely falsified. It was all theater, with me playing the rube that sold it to the rest of the rubes. The coasts—or should I say, the most profitable cities in America—were fine. Were always fine. Were always going to be fine.

I was brought to a hotel by the Servicemen who, as you might've guessed, are the same Old-America operatives guiding the general flow of things on the inside. They made me a deal— continue playing ball in an expanded role keeping the center of America penned up in exchange for the safe extraction of my wife and kid. I agreed and they moved me here, to San Francisco, Tech capital of the world. The transition was rough, but I survived.

I explain all of this to one Ms. Riley Owen, who's sitting on the carpet of my inner sanctum of New American television, as I sometimes call it. An aide has come along to clean up her vomit and give her a glass of water and a mint. Her eyes struggle to focus on one image at a time and I get the sense that she hasn't been paying much attention to my great tell-all confession. She chokes half the water down and sucks on the mint. She looks at me like I'm some kind of Wizard of Oz. She's fixated more on the government surveillance than historical revisionism. Well, I can see with the life that she's led that that might be the bigger priority.

"I suppose you'd rather want the explanation, for... all this?" I gesture at the walls of the room and then pat my console, with feigned affection.

Riley nods.

"Well, why don't I show you. Let's see. Oh yes, Riley, do you remember the Frontmen biker that you whipped to the ground with your dog chain?"

Riley looks at the ceiling of her head.

"Yeah," she says, no longer thinking, but not looking at me.

I spin a dial and flip a couple of switches. The television screens flip to the a streetlight's perspective of Riley grappling the handlebars of a motorbike before twisting the chain and then letting go. Riley and Clay escape but the camera lingers on the injured gentlemen crawling from his bike's wreckage. He's half on his feet before he's fed into the tires of a braking trucker.

Riley doesn't have a whole lot to say about that.

I say, "That guy's name is..." I plug a number into my console and turn a dial. "Oh yes, Josh Vaniski. I've watched him grow up. He burst a kiddie pool when he was seven years old because he was too fat. He developed a neurosis about it, I think." That's a bit of a guess. I'm not a psychologist— I just sit here watching TV and come up with my own theories on what people are feeling. "But I know that when he entered high school, or the remnants of the educational system, at 'teenaged' this guy burrowed into his own hate. He didn't join the Frontmen for any ideological reasons. He just wanted an excuse to bust open some skulls. He was a monster in high school. You want to know what he did?"

Riley isn't sure she wants to know. The look on her face, in the screen, and in person, shows that she wants the justification I'm about to give her. But she also wants vindication. And that's slightly different. Because I can't give that to her. I *can* give her something else. I hit a couple buttons and a movie plays on one of the screens:

It's Josh Vaniski. Fifteen years old. He's already eaten his portioned corn meal and cheese for lunch. Riley can see him hunched over awkwardly at his table, alone and hungry. I watch Riley watch Josh. She can see his eyes dart around to pick a victim— maybe that's unfair to Josh. Maybe he sees the food first. And then he appraises the potential target— size vs. portion, opportunity and reward.

Josh launches towards a student, who's actually taller than him, and throws the grits and cheese to the ground. Then he sizes up to one of the victim's friends, both of them shaking scared. Josh happens to throw the first punch, a lucky shot, a knockout on the jaw. The tall boy checks on his friend as Josh picks up the plate of food and begins to run while shoving cornmeal into his mouth.

Riley leaps forward to shut the video video off. She looks surprised that she did it. I smile.

"It's a lot harder when you have to see them as people, isn't it?" I ask. "But rest assured he was a tyrant. A better world spins on without him."

Riley says nothing. Casually, I return to the console and plug in a sequence.

On the screen: Riley's thirteen years old, crying outside of a burning house. She's not alone. She holds a dog close to her chest.

"I've known you a long time, Riley," I say, as soothingly as I can.

"Turn it off, turn it off!" Riley screams.

The dog struggles, attempting to break free from Riley's grasp and head towards the blaze to search for its other owners. The look in Riley's eyes know that the effort would be futile. She's seen the fury of the Forgiveness firsthand.

"And I want you to know that I wish you no harm."

"Turn it off," Riley chokes, between struggled gasps for breath.

On screen, Riley doesn't cry. She just holds onto the dog and watches her house burn into a funeral pyre for her parents.

"Off," she repeats one final time before collapsing on the floor.

I watch her, waiting until her regular breathing returns. She looks a little like a beaten dog on the floor, wrapped in chains, wearing her frayed and tattered clothes. I know, perhaps more than anybody, more than the other former, voyeuristic presidents, that this dog's had a hard road. Let her sleep.

He that sleeps feels not the tooth-ache.

A Serviceman comes by at my request to quarter her in a spare room upstairs and I return to my whiskey and my duty, watching a million dogs sleep in a big, big kennel.

Breakfast of Champions

Breakfast at the O'Brien household is a quiet affair. Denny O'Brien ploughs through his scrambled eggs, bacon and toast like a lion tearing through the belly of a gazelle. Riley doesn't touch her plate and just sits there, looking rattled. She has only been awake for twenty minutes, having slept in her clothes in the guest bed upstairs. I myself am not present at the table.

I watch from my corridor of screens, theirs just one example of America eating breakfast amongst millions.

Once finished eating, Denny asks, "Not hungry?"

Riley responds by shaking her head. Denny takes her plate and starts with the bacon. She watches Denny demolish her food with delight. Bacon and Eggs. A classic. Denny's favorite. We used to take him to the chain restaurant of his namesake, back when they were still a thing. I guess he attached to the memories.

Riley says, "Don't know how you can eat like that straight out of the hospital."

Denny winks. "Spend a night in a hospital sometime. You'll work up an appetite."

Riley smiles and looks at her hands. Her voice cracks.

"You're Clyde O'Brien's son." Just like that, without having to ask. A mere statement of fact.

"Yep. Him's my pop." He speaks while eating and nearly chokes on his orange juice. Honestly, that kid sometimes.

"So when you stood up for me in the desert, you... you threatened that man to have his sister-in-law deported."

"Yep."

"Deported... to where I came from?"

"Inside, that's right."

"So it's like, what? A prison? Where I'm from?"

"I wouldn't call it a prison." Denny burps. "More like a Third World country."

"And you, or rather, your dad has the power to put people in... the New States."

"There's a bit of a process to it, but yeah. In extreme cases, that's what happens."

"How is that..."

"Legal?"

Riley clears her throat. "Yeah."

"It basically works as if everyone's from the New States. Everyone here on the Outside Ring has, what you might call a visa. Your visa expires if you, say, don't pay your taxes or go unemployed for too long..."

"If you hold certain political views?"

Denny looks disgusted. "That's... that doesn't happen."

"How can you be sure?"

"Because deportations don't happen very often. People are happy here. They comply."

"Or they're afraid of going Inside?"

"Who wouldn't be? Are you going to argue that it's better in there than it is out here?"

"No," Riley muses. "But the fact that people killing each other out of tribal loyalties Inside is being used as criminal deterrence out here... it's distressing."

"It's not a perfect system, I'll give you that."

"Then why not make the Inside a better place to live? Why the wall at all?"

Denny shrugs. "I guess people don't think its worth it. Or they're too involved with their own lives to care, so long as they don't have to put up with it." Denny drops his fork. For once. "Listen, I get you, I really do. It all looks pretty unfair, but that's just how it is. It's how it *needs* to be." He picks up his fork again. "For now, at least."

Riley stands to get herself a cup of coffee. Her stunned expression settles into one of slight amusement.

"Heh." She sips her coffee. "They don't care."

Riley plops back into her chair, spilling a bit of coffee on the table. She wipes at it with her sleeve. She looks at Denny.

"Do you care? About the Inside? About the people

there?"

Denny stops eating and looks her straight in the eyes.

"I usually don't give it a whole lot of thought." He rubs his forehead. "When I do, I just sort of get a little sad, but really, it's not my reality. Tell you the truth, you're kind of the first person I've met from the New States. People go in. They don't usually come out."

"You did."

"Yeah," Denny smiles. "I did. Brought you with me."

"I guess I should thank you for that."

"They were going to kill you."

"I know."

"No thanks necessary. Just thought I'd do the right thing." Denny puts his hand on Riley's.

"Didn't say I was thanking you. Just said I should." Riley pulls out her hand, let slip another *heh* and rests her palm gently over Denny's knuckles.

Her hand has become red and slick. Deep red. Riley stares at it, not even shocked yet. The shock hits her in the gut. The blood coats her hand, and is spilling out onto the table. The source: Denny's mouth gushes a crimson waterfall. His eyes are a cloudy pink, the pupils aiming towards Heaven. Riley stands, knocking the chair over behind her. She stifles a scream. Denny makes a gurgling noise from somewhere between his stomach and throat and spasms to the floor. The blood from his mouth has turned pink with foam.

Riley hyperventilates as she kneels down to Denny and clutches his hand. Denny clutches back. The death rattle shakes loose the final seconds of Denny's life and suddenly he's a limp doll in a puddle of his own blood and vomit. His hand releases its grip from Riley's. She looks at him in horror and pity and confusion. At first she thinks this is a continued episode of the previous day's seizure. Then she realizes otherwise. Her eyes fling open as a shuddering chill resonates through her vertebrae.

He ate my breakfast. Oh, God. He ate my breakfast.

She hears the front door open and close.

Weapon. I need a weapon.

She grabs a blood covered fork from the ground, a bit of egg still in the prongs. She hears two sets of foot steps walking down the hall.

Not enough. Need something else. A knife, something, please!

She grabs Denny's orange juice glass.

"Hello?" says a familiar voice call from the hall. "Enjoying breakfast?" A snicker follows.

Riley stuffs herself into the cupboard under the sink. A bottle of cleaning agent bursts and begins to burn the skin of her midriff. Through a crack she sees two people step into the kitchen: Gene, the Serviceman who nearly put a bullet in Riley's head in the desert, and the female Serviceman who laughed at Riley's fear of the ocean. They're dressed in the same soldier garb from when she last saw them.

Gene smiles as he walks to the body on the floor. But when it begins to dawn on him what happened this morning, Gene looks like a balloon about to pop. The female soldier puts a hand to her mouth, coughs through her revulsion. Her eyes are shielded by aviators, but Riley can tell her eyes are closed as if trying to shake off a bad dream.

"Shit!" cries Gene. "Shit! Shit! Shit! Denny... oh shit, Ky, oh shit."

Ky gets her bearings and stands straight. She says, "Is she here? She escaped."

Gene, pacing now with his hands on his head, says, "Is *he* home. Did he watch this? He knows what happened. We're screwed, Ky. We're dead."

"You killed the president's son," Ky says, without emotion.

"You helped," says Gene. "We had to. He... hold on... *She's...* she can't be here. She can go back, tell everyone. She'd ruin everything. We did it, Ky. And we had to." Gene fumbles for a cigarette. "We were asked to."

"She did it," Ky says. "She poisoned him. We can find the tape. Make it disappear. Maybe Clyde hasn't seen it yet."

Gene takes a deep, lung-lacerating drag. He says, "She's still on the loose. What happened here. Think. Think... Denny eats the poisoned food. He falls over dead. We didn't see anyone from the street leave this house."

"She's still here."

"She's still here," Gene confirms. A wicked grin wraps around his mouth.

Riley's teeth are clamped against each other, lest she

make a noise. But she can't keep from shaking. A soft jingle from her chains gives her up. Ky's ears perk up. She points her rifle at the cupboard under the sink. Gene shakes his head and puts a finger up to his lips. Ky shoulders the rifle and removes the knife from its sheath. Gene nods, his sick smile still twisting his features.

Ky crouches down and gently pulls open the cupboard door.

"I found yo—AAAUGHK."

Riley shoves the fork into Ky's open mouth as far as it will go and keeps pushing until it plunges through the back of her throat. Ky falls on her knees, splutters on blood, retching and choking. Blood and tears wet her face as she tries to pull the fork out, screaming vowels.

Riley knocks Ky on her back with a rabbit punch to the throat as she moves for Gene. Gene's got his pistol unholstered by the time Riley's on the table. She gets it out of his hand with a lash from her dog leash. Gene reaches for his knife as Riley falls into him, juice glass raised over her head like a dagger. She brings it down into his forehead, and forces Gene onto the floor. The rim of the glass chips and breaks against the resistance of Gene's thick skull, but Riley keeps pushing. Gene's eyes are red mirrors. His hands try to repel her from him, but they can't quite coordinate and he flails helplessly. Riley doesn't stop until the bottom of the glass is flush with Gene's skin.

Gene says, "Sizzle. Bounce. Home. Dog," before emitting a low register howl, followed by a moan, followed by nothing at all.

Riley picks up Gene's fallen cigarette from the floor. It's dead, wet with blood. She searches Gene's pockets for his pack and lighter. She stands up, walks to the table sits back down at the place where she was sharing a quiet breakfast with a nice idiot just ten minutes ago. She lights up and puts her elbows on the table.

There's a ringing in her ears— adrenaline flushing out of her system— so it takes her a moment to comprehend the other noise in the room.

Ky's only managed to shove the fork deeper into her throat. Her face is slathered in white and red and orange and brown. The fork handle chatters against broken teeth. Riley sees her, and Ky sees Riley. Ky crawls towards her rifle. Riley steps on Ky's wrist.

"You going to kill me with that?" Riley asks, bottom row of teeth showing. Ky chokes in response.

"Sit still," Riley says. She puts a foot on Ky's head and bends down to reclaim her fork. It's a twist and yank job. Riley looks at the pink meat stuck in the prongs.

Heh.

Ky takes a wet gasp, finally getting a full dose of oxygen, and enough blood into her lungs to finally suffocate. Riley smokes as Ky craters into an agonized sleep: the time between spasms lengthens, Ky's muscles tighten, and there's no frequency of breath other than inhale, inhale, inhale…

Riley rests against the table, smoking her cigarette and looking around the room with no particular focus. There isn't a single inch of the kitchen that isn't tainted red with blood.

Riley watches it all turn brown.

Big Day Out

Picture a stolen car. Stolen from where? The parking lot of a Spokane bar. Why the bar and not one of the vehicles outside of Scum Haus? Easy. Clay fancied a home to come back to and preferred to keep certain feathers unruffled. What kind of car? How about a Rabbit coupe with a broken sunroof that won't roll back into place. Picture Clay gunning the gas while trying to learn how to drive stick on the fly. Got it? It's a herky-jerky, stalling bad time. Now imagine Zeph, the teenaged Scum gunman, leaning out of the window, placing bullets in the tires of pursuant drunk-driven jeeps.

Clay works the clutch and re-shifts and the Rabbit flies down the road, no time to downshift to accommodate the upcoming turns— Clay throws his own weight opposite of the fishtail and nearly bucks Zeph out of the window before he corrects course as the road straightens. A bullet slaps a spider web on the rear windshield. Zeph's out the window again and plucks a gunner from his seat. He eases back into his seat, nonplussed, and calmly reloads cartridges into his pistol.

Clay's known Zeph for about two hours and already knows the following about his new companion— he doesn't rattle, he came to Spokane by way of Northern Texas, his family got clipped by the Forgiveness during one for their Crusades into the South, his favorite breakfast is steak and eggs, and he is an absolute fiend with a gun. Clay's not sure whether to respect or fear Zeph and unsure if there's a difference between the two. But Clay also knows that Zeph volunteered to join him on this mission without any cajoling and figures that means he's got something akin to a soul behind those cold, dead eyes of his. Zeph's Scum, through and through, but as Zeph himself said:

"That don't mean alignment to nothing, not even jamming up other Scum. The Rat King might eat himself, given he's desperate enough."

Out the window with Zeph again, six shots fired in a hurry, like he wasn't even aiming. Clay checks his rearview to see a jeep skid into a ditch.

The mission is, of course, to find that missing nuclear launch console, and stop Patrick and Carly from... whatever the hell it is that they think they're doing.

Leads: none to speak of, other than the knowledge that Patrick and Carly are booze-swilling Scum dogs. Which means that they'd probably make a stop or two at a gas station or super market to either buy or lift beer. Another theory, Zeph's: in addition to alcohol, Patrick and Carly would probably want to get their hands on less popular yet somewhat easily obtainable intoxicants. That means nitrous oxide canisters, which meant restaurant supply stores and pornography chains.

But first, the remaining riffraff: still one jeep in the rearview. Zeph out the window again with the six shooter, pops three before the gun jams. Up ahead: a 90 degree turn. Zeph unloads and inspects the chamber. Clay fumbles the gears and locks the clutch— stalls. The jeep smashes into the back of the Rabbit, hurling a drunk through his windshield and into the rear Rabbit window, punching a hole through the spiderweb with his face. He's pretty dead. The gunner riding shotgun in the jeep has his elbow bent the wrong way. Problem solved. Clay untangles the gears, hits the clutch and lurches forth, regulating a decent speed once again, this time with zero pissed-off drunks in his rearview.

Zeph navigates, having a cursory knowledge of the general area. The first stop, a liquor store. The description of Patrick and Carly invites a shotgun to the conversation. A good lead. It proves Patrick and Carly stopped to boost liquor— that means they were on the right trail. But there were three directions branching from there. According to Zeph: north rounds back towards Scum Haus, east towards a gas station where they could've filled up their car and boosted some beer, south holds a gas station *and* a porn shop. It'd be south if

Pat and Carly were feeling lucky enough to rip off three stores in a row. And you'd feel pretty goddamn lucky if you had a nuclear trigger riding bitch.

South it is.

No go on the gas station. Clay fights the urge to flip northeast and check the other, but Zeph insists on the porn store. It's a mess. Magazines and videotapes litter the ground outside. It's a worse scene inside. A clerk with a flat, bloody nose confirms the store was robbed by a man and a woman who cleaned out all of their poppers and nitrous. He chases Clay and Zeph out with a baseball bat after too many questions. Bingo.

Where to next? Follow the mentality of the Rat King. Zeph's the divining rod.

Pat and Carly are loaded up and bogged down by chemicals. Only makes sense they'd try and justify their high with powerful stimulants.

Clay: "Where could they have scored some meth or coke?"

Zeph: "There's a truck stop 30 miles east of here."

Clay guns it, floods it, clutches it and then takes off.

They rip right into Idaho, old Neo-Nazi strongholds, current methamphetamine circuits, juice strong enough to fuel truckers from Montana to Alabama, no sleep. Pat and Carly would have to play nice to barter for drugs here. You come off as too agressive and you're lumped in with the cargo and dropped into the Mississippi while passing through St. Louis. Come off as too skiddish and you're lucky if they let you die. Speed demons and their speed don't let the slightest wedge between them and they're all tight with each other. Clay and Zeph don't even need to play it a certain way. There's too much carnage.

A semi on its side, having crushed a public toilet. One semi lodged into the cargo of another. Pills, vials and syringes cracking under foot and tire like gravel. Carly's hatchback wedged under a tire, entirely burnt out and pluming smoke. Heavy bearded men running around, some with knives, others with guns, trying to get a handle on things. Prostitutes huddled on the grass, passing cigarettes and pints of liquor.

Zeph groks the scene: Pat and Carly ran a kamikaze-distraction mission. Probably unloaded the bomb down road ahead of time. Then wheeled back, lit the hatchback ablaze and let it ride empty with a brick on the gas pedal into an idling truck, the ensuing pandemonium leaving a lot of cabs empty as drivers checked out the scene—Pat got into a truck and trashed it, Carly did the same, erstwhile grabbing the glovebox stashes. They ducked out, and with the fresh chaos, ran the same scheme again, wrecking a semi each before hopping into a fifth semi, together, to grab the nuclear package and blow further east.

The Rabbit elicits some attention as it circles through the truck stop. Some men posture, aiming rifles and side arms. Zeph shoots the cigarette out of the mouth of a mountain-shaped man. Another raises a shotgun— Zeph puts a bullet through the barrel, ignites the shells on impact. The man's minus a finger and the message is received. The Rabbit rolls on east, best as Clay can manage. The ground outside trades its dismal yellow and gray dirt for white and blue snow.

Not too many places Pat and Carly could've headed at this point. With a semi-truck, they couldn't have gone through the back roads, they'd've backed into a ditch. And with the snow coming down— *snow?* Thinks Clay. *In July? Is the weather broken?* It isn't, but it's not a great omen. They're piecing together a cracked out fantasy now. Clay thinks the transition to a semi means Missoula would be the next logical stop. Zeph's not so sure.

Rat King philosophy: "You only eat what you can take."

Meaning Pat and Carly bit off more than they could chew. Why bother driving a semi when you could flip it, stall two lanes of traffic, snag a car off of some sucker trying to make it back to Coeur d'Alene? That'd jam up the speedo trucker Nazis on your tail, hide your tracks, and still somehow aid the bigger, demented picture. They fly on down the road, keeping a lookout for anything out of the ordinary.

Wouldn't you know it. Traffic jam. Zeph's sure of his hypothesis. Only thing now is to ditch the Rabbit and schlep their box of ammunition and cans of roast beef hash down the parade of stalled cars.

Zeph leads, pistol barrel to the ground like a proper soldier. Angry honks. Freezing commuters. Overheating cars. Three quarters of a mile's worth of snowy footprints and they see the truck capsized as predicted. It would require some footwork in the woods to get around it and back on the road. A mile of headlights ahead.

Zeph: sharklike, wants to keep swimming.

Clay: beat. Wants to stop. Takes the excuse for rest as an investigative instinct. Check the cab of the overturned semi. Zeph standing guard, Clay climbing wheels. Slips. Grease on his hands. Hauls over. Pops open the door.

Patrick. Half-strangled by seat belts against the grounded window. Two sticks in his arm. Dopey grin on his face. Beer in his hand.

Clay thinks he's dead at first. Patrick laughs. Starts spewing Rat King nonsense.

"A rat'll loose himself from the king only by chewing away at his own tail."

Pat shakes off enough delirium to recognize Clay.

"Ah, my friend." Patrick grabs at Clay's foot, tries to put it in a headlock. He chokes a little bit in the effort. "Bruise, my friend. You're here!"

Clay says, "I'm here, Patrick. Where's Carly?"

"Carly and me got to thinking," Patrick says, pouring an ounce of beer into his mouth. "We got to thinking, and I've had this thought for a long time, that society, the world..." Patrick drags his head to the right and then the left. "That the world can't have us. It's unacceptable. Who wants a world of Rat Kings reigning supreme? We're SCUM."

"I know we are, I know we are," says Clay.

"Nobody," slurs Patrick. He appears to fall asleep but comes awake with a sniff. "*NOBODY* wants a world of rats. You know what they do? You know what they do. They exterminate. Me and Carly had a thought. A fanciful, fly-by, happy-go-lucky-thought." Patrick giggles in pink bubbles. "Exterminate the humans... and let the rest become rats. Like us." Patrick hiccups. "And then we'll build anew. That's what's good about it, right? It won't look all polished and shiny... but it'll be new. It'll be equal. And then... oh boy." Patrick vomits.

Clay reasons, "But people will die. A lot of people. Just because we're divorced from the world doesn't mean that we still can't do our own thing. It doesn't mean we need to engage the others at all!"

Patrick: more Rat King gibberish.

"The Rat King is a symptom of disease. Either the disease dies or the body carrying the disease dies. Makes no difference to me."

And with that, Patrick eases into his broken glass pillow and dons a smile of contentment, backstroking away from the chaos he wrought and accepting graciously the gift of non-participation. His breath stops. Clay checks his pulse. Dead.

Clay takes the beer out of his hand, takes a small sip, and then overturns the can onto Patrick, a foamy stream of domestic lager to get Patrick's ghost to where it needed going.

A Scum funeral.

Carly taught him that.

Lights, Camera, Axe

Chicago, the windy city. The last 30 years have not been kind. Power grids checker the downtown area, alternating light and dark every other block. Reeve knows that there's a strong Frontier enclave here, even a Frontmen chapter. But he also knows's it's ringed by Good Old Americans and plagued with pockets of nondenominational criminal gangs. Right now, it's quiet, cold, and not all that windy.

Unlike Salt Lake City, where the streets were orderly under the martial law of the Just, Chicago's streets are trashed with newspapers, refuse and broken glass. Homeless encampments are built in the middle of intersections. The Frontier, it would seem, maintains a power hold of the area by hoarding space in the high rises, the towers, only sending out foot soldiers to the streets to quash immediate threats or to protect a select few aligned businesses. They left the bottom world to rot.

"Cowards," spits Reeve. "Ghosts in their own city."

A glass bottle splinters against the hood of their car. A shadow runs into an alleyway. Rebecca pumps her shotgun.

"Easy, Becky," Reeve says. "They're just pissed that we have a car. They probably see it as a status thing." He hits the windshield wipers to brush away shards

"I'd be pissed, too," says Xavier.

"You can't let these animals walk all over you like that," Rebecca snarls. "And don't *ever* call me Becky."

"They're not animals," says Reeve. "They're just people choked to desperation."

"So was I," says Rebecca. "I got out. I got a job."

"Yeah, well, not everyone is so lucky are they?" grits Reeve.

"Not everyone is so pretty either," says Xavier.

Rebecca tickles Xavier's ear with the shotgun.

"Don't talk to me." She leans in to say, "At all."

Reeve angles the car around a homeless tent camp. A running car draws a lot of stares and a few beggars asking for food. Reeve waves and mouths a sad "no, sorry," to them. Every time the beggar nods and says "God bless." Except for one who bares her teeth menacingly.

Reeve pulls up to a nondescript brick apartment building, four stories, in Northside. He shakes his head and rounds the block looking for the same address. He finds the apartment again. He tools around the entire neighborhood, thinking there must be a mistake, but they always end up at the same spot.

"That doesn't look like much," Xavier says, scanning the facade of the building. "Looks like a dumpy apartment building."

"Rent must be low," says Reeve.

"Hiding in plain sight," says Rebecca. "A building like this is outside of the reach of the Frontier— they'd've stolen the lease of a nicer place."

"I imagined a warehouse or something."

"Couldn't be exactly ground level, could it?" says Rebecca. "That's a security risk. Needs to be at least on a second story. Hardly anyone would think to look here."

"Except your average, run-of-the-mill thieves."

"Which I'm sure they could dispatch without an issue." Rebecca tightens her grip on her shotgun. "Or without raising too much suspicion."

"So there's armed guards inside," says Reeve.

"Likely," confirms Rebecca.

"Do we have a plan?" asks Xavier. Rebecca sighs and unzips a leather satchel from the floor. She takes out Reeve and Xavier's modified pistols and hands them across the car.

"You go in first. You turn more than 70 degrees towards me, I cut you in half. Got it?"

"Got it," says Xavier.

Reeve is hesitant. "Our plan is to literally just throw the door down and go in guns a-blazing?"

Rebecca says, "Yep."

"I don't like it," says Reeve.

"I hate it," says Xavier.

"The door has *got* to be reinforced."

"Padlocked."

"And guarded."

Rebecca sighs. "If you have another idea, I'd love to hear it."

Xavier has an idea. He leads the other two out of the car, Rebecca in rear leveling the shotgun at Reeve's tailbone.

Her warning: "Just remember, if I have to shoot you, I'll make sure you'll live a lot longer than you'd like."

Xavier leads them up the steps and to the front door. There's a keypad under the knob, but Xavier hazards that it doesn't do anything. He's right. Next: four flights of stairs, involving a lot of stepping over vagrants and drunks on tippy-toes, lest they wake anyone and give away their position. On the fourth floor, they locate the apartment number Fulter had given them— a piece of intel he'd been working for months to attain. Xavier motions for the other two to keep going— and he stops in front of the neighboring apartment.

He knocks. Twice.

No answer. He tries the knob. Locked. Judging by the way the door budges, he discerns that there's a deadbolt in his way. Which means that they can't kick it down— they wouldn't want to, as it would cause too much ruckus. So would forcing the door open with a crowbar.

He needs a lock pick.

The three do a silent inventory search. Reeve rabbit-ears his pockets and comes up with a couple of coins, a cigarette lighter and lint. Xavier turns to Rebecca.

"Do you have any bobby pins?"

Rebecca takes off her skull cap, exposing a shaved scalp.

"Damn." Says Xavier. "Reeve, give me your belt. And a nickel."

"Why?" Reeve asks in a harsh whisper.

"Please?"

Reeve unbuckles his belt and hands it over. Xavier pries the prong from the buckle and hands the belt back.

"Oh, come on," says Reeve, re-looping his belt. His pants sag.

Xavier inserts the prong into the keyhole and gently knocks the pins of the lock upwards, one after the other. After the third, he inserts the nickle and twists, slowly rotating the cylinder.

Click

The three shuffle inside the room. Reeve hits a light. Much of the apartment has been burnt out.

"Either a minor gas explosion, or a hobo fire," guesses Rebecca.

"Could've been drug manufacturing gone awry," whistles Reeve. "Amateurs."

Xavier scans the walls for electrical outlets. He finds two along the western wall. He explains:

"We want to find the weakest part of the wall with as

few obstructions between us and the other side as possible. For example, we couldn't do this in the bathroom because there's too many pipes. You can't do it over an electrical outlet, because there's likely to be electrical wire and tight studs in the way. But between outlets…"

"There shouldn't be too much of anything," finishes Reeve.

Xavier looks to Rebecca to see if she's impressed. She's not. Yet.

"We doing the Boise Boy Breakthrough?" asks Reeve.

"Absolutely," Xavier says. "Reeve, if you'd be so kind… The kitchen, perhaps?."

"Right." Reeve goes to the kitchen, or what's left of the rotten chamber containing a refrigerator and stove range, and looks through the cupboards until he finds a cast-iron frying pan. He brings it back to the living room.

"This work?" he asks.

"Should be perfect," says Xavier. "Be sure to go quickly. We have maybe three seconds before they start shooting back."

"That should be enough."

"What's going on?" Rebecca asks. "I'm not used to not understanding the plan."

Xavier pulls a piece of charred wood from the floor and uses it to draw a target on the wall.

"Rebecca, if you would be so kind as to fire that shotgun three times directly into this area from a distance of six feet, we'd be very grateful."

"What?"

"Fire three times. Very quickly. No more than three though, because Reeve here is going to jump into your line of fire to finish the job."

Rebecca says, "I don't—"

"Shoot the goddamn gun!" yells Reeve.

Rebecca pumps the action, fires, pumps, fires, pumps, fires. The wall is grated swiss cheese. Reeve jumps in with the cast iron, swinging away at drywall and splintered wood. Three seconds. Reeve ducks. Xavier lunges into the newly made hole in the wall and wedges halfway through to the other side, gun raised. He puts a bullet in the chin of the guard by the door. Another in the shoulder and stomach of a startled guard sitting on a chair, his pornographic magazine in ribbons. Xavier pushes through the wall, coughing out white dust. Reeve isn't far behind him, looking similarly antiquated in powdered drywall. The guard slips from his chair to the floor and makes a feeble attempt to reach his fallen gun under the coffee table. Reeve pops his forehead with the frying pan, sending the man on his back.

Gary Denilles, the math whiz, the genius behind the voting machine, the target Fulter gave Reeve and Xavier to kill, drops a bowl of macaroni and cheese and bolts for the front door. Like Xavier predicted, it was padlocked, and takes a couple of seconds to unlock. Gary opens the door to find Rebecca's shotgun pointed squarely at his nose. She scrapes Gary's eye glasses with the muzzle.

"Howabout we turn that ass around towards that chair over there."

Rebecca marches Gary to the bloody lounge chair. Gary's guard is shocked in pain on the floor, still alive. Reeve puts a bullet through the poor guy's head to end the suffering, eyes on Denilles. Rebecca takes a seat on the couch.

"Any more goons?" she asks.

Denilles shakes his head.

Reeve asks, "The studio?"

Denilles says, "Past the kitchen, second door on your right."

Xavier goes to check it out. It's a converted bedroom, black drop cloths over the windows, foam sheets covering the walls, a camera in one corner, the notorious voting machine in the other. Xavier inspects the machine, tapping its plastic case with his finger. It sounds hollow. Xavier leaves the room and checks out the other bedroom: mattress, books, flatscreen monitor with an electrocardiogram next to the current President's name — currently blank. Xavier closes that door, too.

Xavier walks up to Gary Denilles and puts his gun to his head.

He says, playfully, "You're not really a mathematician, are you?"

"I am," Gary swears, "I am."

"But the machine's a fake."

"It is, it's a fake. Shit, don't shoot."

Reeve says, "We're supposed to kill you, you know. If I

were you, I'd start explaining a few things."

Denilles says, "It's true that I was a math professor. That looked good for them. Good enough. I got approached by certain men." Denilles straightens his shirt with a flat palm, eyes to the ground. "They said I could protect my family. Jesus, the way things were… I told them I'd do it. If I knew… if I knew that I was just sending men and women to their deaths, I would've… I would've… I don't know. What would you have done?"

No one has a response to that.

"How's it work?" asks Rebecca.

"Ch-chain of command," stutters Denilles. "There's a heart monitor in my room. It displays the heart beat of the current president elect. We know the exact moment his heart stops. When it does, and it almost always stops, I get a phone call with the next name."

"Damn. So Fulter was right about the node implants," says Reeve.

"It's a quick procedure done shortly after birth. If not then, then sooner or later everyone has to go to the hospital for one reason or another."

"Who get's picked?"

"Sometimes it is random, just to keep up appearances. But by and large it's a prominent member of a dissident faction or people who've learned too much. You know as well as I do, that getting elected is almost a certain death sentence. This machine ensures that organizations stay scrambled and political parties remain antagonistic to each other."

"But some people actually become president."

"Yes, that's true. They go to a little place in Nebraska and stooge as president for a year. If they're successful, they're rewarded with the safety of their family and extraction from this hell hole." Denilles releases a tense sigh. "There's a job waiting for them on the other side."

Reeve jabs at Denilles's shoulder with his gun.

"Extraction? Other side?"

This confuses Denilles at first. "I thought you'd have figured it out by now."

"Assume we're playing dumb to hear you say it."

"Extraction to the coasts. They were never bombed to oblivion like you thought. D.C. fell, but governmental organization persisted on the East Coast in New York City and on the West Coast in San Francisco. There are a few other satellite cities of power, such that no one city controls everything."

"If one falls, the whole country doesn't fall apart," muses Rebecca. "Good strategy."

Reeve takes a seat and rubs his temples. Xavier twirls his gun around his finger while he paces around the room in slow, lofty strides. Denilles continues.

"Clyde O'Brien was fed a series of executive orders by the Outer Ring, as they began calling it. O'Brien dictated that the Inner Circle would be walled-off, as you know. Followed by making air travel illegal and furthermore impossible by bulldozing every single airport in the Circle. And subverting the efforts of those with enough capital and education from reforming aviation technology. Well, most technologies, to be blunt. I'm afraid the Inner Circle is about 20 years behind the Outer Ring."

Reeve chews on his thumbnail bitterly while glaring at Denilles. Xavier inhales and exhales loudly. He can't seem to stop shaking his head.

Rebecca puts her shotgun to Denilles's kneecap. "Now tell us why."

"Why? Simple. After it was clear that the majority of Americans were capable of razing Washington D.C. to the ground and publicly executing the sitting President, containment measures needed to be enacted. It's the same reason why a live wire will be re-routed into itself to be contained as a circuit that does nothing, instead of unreliably patched into a greater network."

A silence falls over the living room with the exception of Reeve chomping on his thumbnail. Denilles licks his lips and looks as if he's about to ask for a glass of water. He's been speaking for a long time.

"Why not just kill us all?" asks Xavier.

"Industry," says Denilles, his voice cracking. "Millions of workers, starving to make a dime. There's plenty of farm goods produced here, aren't there? A little bit of oil. Manufacturing." Denilles coughs. "Industry can persist anywhere, despite tumultuous conditions. So the local economy between states are still allowed. Some is even encouraged with outside money and resources. But you'd never see where 70% of the stuff goes. As far as not killing everybody and invading…" Denilles adjusts his glasses and mumbles, "People have a habit of reproducing rather quickly."

"Why believe you?" asks Reeve.

"I've got no reason to lie to you now that you killed my guards. I was forced into this job because my family's life was put to hazard, in addition to my own." Denilles flexes his fingers together nervously. "Now it seems like it doesn't really matter. You're going to kill me aren't you?"

"I've got an idea," says Xavier. "You can put any name into the lottery and elect that person as president, right?"

"The machine is just old vacuum parts and an empty computer. I just say the name on the air and people believe me."

"Michael Fulter," says Rebecca. "Elect Michael J. Fulter."

"The CEO of Lyla Transistors?" asks Denilles.

"That's the one."

"Wait," says Reeve. "I don't understand. He's your boss, isn't he?"

Rebecca says, "He's my client. I take orders from the Just."

"Why do you want Fulter dead?"

Rebecca sighs.

"We want the same thing, right? Stability? Fulter's a poor excuse for a man who uses a well-organized mercenary army for petty reasons. He didn't want you guys to just kill Denilles, he wanted control of the machine, the power to elect anyone *he* wanted. I'm all for capitalism, but I won't stand for absolute power."

"I don't know," says Xavier. "Your Yellow Jacket buddies are protecting him, after all. They've had a pretty good track record of getting people to Nebraska."

"True," says Rebecca. "But let's just say that I've made a few arrangements with a few trustworthy Yellow Jackets. Besides, do *you* have a problem with electing Fulter? Your choices are between putting a mark on him and having him killed—thus breaking your obligation to him— or killing Denilles, reclaiming the 'voting machine' and bringing it to Fulter, at which point he's likely to hit the kill switch on both of you anyway."

Xavier sits down and thinks pensively. Reeve remains standing and taps his foot rapidly. He doesn't have to consider the options for very long.

"Elect the motherfucker."

Reeve turns to Denilles and says, "In the studio," and gestures with his gun down the hall into the makeshift studio.

Denilles coaches his hitmen on how to set up the lighting and sound equipment. He stands on the taped X next to his voting machine and explains to Xavier how to run the cameras. They go live:

"Good evening, America. As you know, we are looking for another President Elect. So it is with great humility that I consult the voting machine that has kept this democratic process alive for so many years to find out who will be the next leader of this great country."

* * *

Gary Denilles pulls a lever as numbers blip through the screen. Once it stops, Gary says:

"And the next president elect of the New States of America is Michael J. Fulter. I believe he's the C.E.O. of Lyla Transistors in Salt Lake City and I, speaking for the American people as a whole, wish him the greatest success in his term of Presidency. Thank you and goodnight."

Xavier cuts the transmission. Rebecca gives him a nod. He picks up the camera from its tripod and smashes it against the wall. It's Reeve's turn next with the frying pan. He lays into the voting machine sending chunks of mostly empty plastic and glass flying. It surprises him how easy it is to reduce a symbolic machine to nothing. He thinks it would've been a good image to capture on camera. Rebecca smashes the microphone against the floor and crushes it under her boot.

"That felt good," says Xavier.

"We're not done," says Rebecca. "The heart monitor. Show me."

Xavier leads them to the other room. The phone rings incessantly. *BRING-RIING.* The flatscreen monitor now displays Michael Fulter's name. His heart monitor is bleeping and blooping normally.

"Wait for it…" says Rebecca.

The heart rate flatlines with two minutes of patience. As soon as Fulter's dead, Rebecca looses buckshot into the monitor sending a ghost of burnt plastic and circuit smoke to the ceiling. The phone rings. *BRING-RIING.*

BRING-RIING.

Rebecca shoves the shotgun into Denille's stomach. "You say it happened just as it happened, except that you were attacked and coerced to broadcast by the Forgiveness. Pick it up."

BRING-RIING.

Denilles picks up the receiver, sounding distraught.

"Hello? They're gone now. Philip and Sweeny are dead. They had a gun to my head, what could I do? They said they were, I'm not sure... the Forgotten? The Forgiveness. Yes. That's it. They can't have gone far. Ok. Yes. I understand."

Denilles hangs up the phone.

"They're sending Servicemen. They'll be here in four minutes."

Rebecca says, "Grab him by the ankles and drag him to the car."

Denilles says, "But I did what you said!"

"I know. And you'll do what they'll say. We can't trust you. Like you said, you've got no reason to lie anymore. To anybody."

Denilles lip trembles and he falters in his speech. "B-b-but— I did what y-you s-said!"

"Come along, now, you milquetoast bastard," Xavier says cheerfully.

Xavier and Reeve grab an ankle each and drag Denilles behind them. He barely protests after a few moments.

They follow Rebecca down the four flights of stairs. She's not afraid that they'll turn on her as she's just set the Frontmen free with Fulter's execution. She just set herself free, as well as the entirety of the Just's Yellow Jackets. All it took was a mild coup. Rebecca smiles for the first time in a long time.

She's had quite a successful day.

A Lean and Hungry Look

Riley sips coffee. The caffeine doesn't help the tremor in her hands or settle the vacuum in her stomach. The adrenaline dump is over and now her body is footing the bill. She breathes slowly to register the shock. She goes over some options.

I can go back to bed and pretend to be asleep. A sip of coffee. *Nope, that's just a stay of execution.* A louder slurp of coffee.

It's quiet. Quiet enough to hear myself think. Where is everybody?

She's afraid to check the house for guards, or, at least she's afraid that they'll see *her* covered in three types of blood. She won't find any Servicemen. I've made sure.

Riley decides on a short-term course of action, which is to put the mug in the sink and run water into it, dump it out and place it on the drying rack. She washes her hands with soap and water. She steps over the body of Ky and leaves the kitchen entirely. She walks down the hall and, noticing that her she's trailing bloody footprints on the hardwood, removes her socks. She goes back up the stairs and into the bathroom. She strips and hangs her clothes and dog chains on a towel rack by the door. She turns on the shower and gets in, letting the cold water jolt her out of shock before it gets warm. She shampoos her hair and scrubs the blood from her arms and face. She gets out of the shower, towels off, wipes the fog from the mirror and inspects herself. Her arms and face are still tinged an orangish-pink. *Will all great Neptune's ocean wash this blood clean from my hand?*

Riley looks at her soaked clothes hanging from the rack. She leaves them there, save for a single dog leash, and looks for alternative vestments. She opens a door just down from her guest bedroom. She finds a young boy's room. Posters of sports heroes, drunk musicians and scantily clad women curl at their edges. An electric guitar collects dust in the corner. This was Denny's room. Riley takes in the atmosphere for a brief moment before feeling as if she's trespassing and quietly closes the door.

The next room is an old office with sparsely decorated walls and a lonely desk without a chair. Riley doesn't stay for long and why would she? No one ever did.

The master bedroom used to belong to Mathilde and myself. The bed is still unmade and probably moist with years of mildewed neglect. On the dresser there are pictures of me and pictures of Mathilde and pictures of

Denny. Her tubes of lipstick and eye shadow. Little bottles of perfume with the tiny squeeze ball… an open purse. Earrings scattered everywhere. I used to holler at her for leaving them just lying around after I stepped on one. Listen to me getting nostalgic. I haven't been there personally for nearly 15 years. Not since they took Mathilde away after my first misstep.

Riley opens the closet and scans for something she can wear. She finds some black tights and shimmies into them. She pulls out a pair of white shorts, the pair Mathilde bought one sunny morning in New Orleans, and fastens it with her leash. She finds a black tank top I don't recognize and pulls her arms and head through. The finishing touch? She takes my beat up, brown leather jacket and slides into it. She runs her hands over the grease stains and cigarette holes. Riley grabs a pair of socks and, before leaving the room, smears a line of garnet lipstick over her mouth. Why not? She *pops* her lips in the mirror and retreats to the door, closing it slowly. She makes a stop in the guest bedroom to put her own shoes on.

Riley descends the staircase, rounds to the hall, avoiding the kitchen— won't even look at it— and pops a head into the living room, again looking for Servicemen. None to speak of. She opens the door to the next set of stairs, descending with fists balled tight, ready for anything.

When she opens the door, she finds a sad old man sitting in his chair, gently strumming a guitar. He sings gently through his damaged vocal chords:

Go ahead and take it all, take it all, take the lot
Never wanted a single thing, never wanted to be king
My only wish was one of peace, and peace ain't what I got
So take the lot and let me be with my lonely song to sing

The old man pauses the song to take a sip of Tennessee sour mash, the finest import from the Inner Circle. He motions to Riley with the pick in his hand. She's looking more than a little confused.

"You like the song?" I ask. She doesn't know how to respond. "That's okay, you don't have to like it. I wrote it, you know. That's all I do down here, really. I sing my little songs and I make my little stories about the little people in the little screens and I try to figure out their little thoughts as they squirrel through their little lives."

There's that spark in Riley's eyes. I wasn't even trying to incite her.

"What do you mean their *little* lives?" she spits.

"They look like ants from down here," I say. I chuckle. I strum an A minor. Such a somber noise. I've always associated it with regret.

"So you just sit down here, drinking, spying on an entire country of people, singing your dumb music."

"Not all my songs are that bad," I say. A smile bleeds into my inflection. Maybe it's just nice to have someone to talk to again. Someone real, for once. I lean into my chair and wave at the corridor of screens. "You watch this show for a couple of decades and you get to learn the tropes a bit. You watch millions of people grow from cradle to grave and it can make you a little callous." I sip Tennessee. "It's not a development that I enjoy about myself."

"You've been doing this for decades? Watching everyone?"

"Oh, I suppose when I started it was more of a radio broadcast. Every street corner bugged, every bar, every school, the homes of certain rambunctious individuals… there was also more of a Servicemen presence in the various factions then. Undercover operatives who'd guide me to the more influential groups and persons. You might recognize a few of them from your history books." I give Riley a wry smile. "Then technology improved and the interest in the Inner Circle waned. I used to have more help. I still have some other eyes and ears, other former Presidents who signed onto a raw deal. But that's bureaucracy for ya, eh?" Another lipful of sweet Tennessee. "So what do I owe the pleasure, Ms. Owen?"

Riley freezes but stands her ground. It's obvious that she doesn't necessarily have a plan.

"I'm here to stop you."

A laugh like a rocket shoots from my stomach, right from where my soul used to hide, out my mouth. Could be the whiskey. I'm in tears.

"Well, where the hell were ya thirty years ago?" My face is in my hand. It's too much. "My dear girl, a-heh, if I could've stopped, I'd've stopped." Hoo-boy. I get a grip.

I strum A minor. "But you're not wrong. You will stop me. Or rather, your fortuitous entrance into this *home* has provided the opportunity for me to stop. For everything to come to a nice, clean end."

Riley grits her teeth. She's the kind of gal who hates being left out of the loop.

She says, "You've got cameras in this house. You watched as my breakfast was poisoned. You did nothing as your son died. You could have stopped it."

"You know that I've watched you since you were a baby, my dear Ms. Owen. I've watched a million people perform their morning routines and people are nothing if not creatures of routine and habit. People might switch it up now and then, but a few things remain static. You, for example, generally don't eat breakfast, favoring two cups of black coffee instead. When you do eat breakfast, you have two pieces of toast with butter if its available. You rarely eat eggs, but when you do, you prefer them poached or soft-boiled."

"What's your point?"

"The point, Ms. Owen, is that you haven't eaten a slice of bacon since you were fourteen years old." Riley's eyes flutter as her mind attempts to register what I've just told her. "So when I ordered Gene and Ky to inject 50 mgs of cyanide into the package of bacon, I knew you'd be safe."

"You…"

"I don't get a whole lot of visits from Denny. He resented his old man the older he became. I don't blame him. He accepted the invitation to come for breakfast this morning to check up on you. Seems you made an impression on him. I was just lucky to see him one last time. You know he hasn't been home in, oh, maybe three or four years."

"You poisoned your son." She says it flat, no longer questioning it.

"It was a little exploitive of Gene, I admit. He saw you as a liability and I leaned on his enthusiasm for your removal. Didn't think he was going to return to watch the show. And what a show it turned out to be!"

"You... Denny... You?"

"Yes, Denny. My greatest accomplishment in life was that boy, despite his more chauvinistic tendencies. Still, I shudder to think what would've happened to him tomorrow. I hate to think of what I did as a favor to him but... well, you already know that I don't enjoy these calluses of mine."

"How could you?"

"I already told you. Oh, you mean, how am I *capable* of killing him. Well, for starters, I had someone else do it. But more to your point, it's not unusual to spare your loved ones from further suffering. Ethical, even."

"You sound like Hitler in his bunker when the Allies were closing in."

"I don't welcome the comparison."

"You don't, maybe, but your actions do."

"I've seen the writing on the wall, Riley. The New States of America isn't sustainable. You can't keep all of the beasts in the Inner Circle. Sooner or later, all hell is going to break loose. I prefer sooner than later, and I'd prefer to not be a part of it any longer. History is going to judge me a certain way and so be it. But I'd rather they not take it out on my progeny. And this little cocktail," I say, jingling the ice in my drink against the glass, "is my indulgent consolation, after failing at just about everything."

"So you're a coward," spits Riley. Venomous words. But the stronger poison has already begun to numb their sting.

"I don't deny it. But I've earned the coward's way out."

Riley scoffs but she's left speechless.

"I may have robbed you of the opportunity for revenge and for that I apologize. But I won't leave you with nothing."

"What could you possibly give me? What could I possibly want from you?"

"I'm going to give you a moment in history. I'm going to leave you alone in a room with camera access to nearly every corner of the New States. I'm going to give you a hint: an old friend still lives and he's crossing through Montana. And then you will be given a choice."

"I don't want it."

"Declining to make a choice is a choice in itself, isn't it?" Flecks of blood accompany a small chuckle. "I've chosen to keep something a secret from the Outer Ring. Something small, but with huge importance. Your old friend is closing in on it. You find him, you'll find what

I'm talking about."

"I don't understand."

"You will. From here on, you'll write the story over all of those little lives."

"I don't want to."

"You don't have to."

"I guess you won't have to, either."

"It's about that time, now. Would you like to hear a story?"

"Not really."

"My last little narration. I'll keep it short."

Riley doesn't say anything. I drink the last of the Tennessee sour mash and smack my lips.

"A little life is born into nowheresville, Georgia. He grows up to become a musician, a husband and a father. And then he becomes the President of the New States of America. He's widowed. He loses his son. He dies. A different story: the Devil jumped up from Georgia to rule the Inner Circle. The Devil has no wife, no children. He doesn't deserve them and work keeps him too busy for a family. The Devil is what I've become and I'm looking forward to tossing the keys to Hell. If I'm lucky, I can die as just Clyde O'Brien."

Riley, of course, doesn't know what to say. But I catch a glint of her eye that has something written in it. It's not forgiveness. I don't want it and wouldn't accept it. It's something not too far from sympathy or possibly it's permission.

I take my eyes from Riley. She needn't be a part of this.

I take a look at myself in the screen. I see an old man, falling slowly from his chair to the floor.

And everything smells like almonds.

Heavy Weigh the Horns

The old man slumps to the floor. Only a trickle of blood leaves his mouth. The coward low-dosed his whiskey so that he wouldn't feel a thing, compared to the gushing red fountain from his son's mouth. His face has relief written into it. Yet his eyes stare at me, as if waiting for me to do something. I remember I'm supposed to do something. But first I drag the old man's body away from the console off into a corner. I don't like the way the blue luminescence of the screens animates the corpse's shadows. When I turn my head, I always think I'm going to catch him moving. But he's dead. No pulse. No life. No more job to do.

And I guess that's where I come in. I ease into his chair. Comfortable— I guess it'd have to be, to have someone sit in it all day, every day, for 30 years. Clyde wanted a replacement. If I play my cards right, I won't have to fit that bill.

I press a few buttons and flip a few switches, getting a feel for how the console works. Fairly simple. A dial switches channels on the screen. A screen holds twenty feeds. A button switches screens to the main display. *Montana... Montana, let's see...* It's kind of exhausting to look at everyone through this technology. It's also appalling. I can see political gatherings in bars and bowling alleys, churches and schools. They don't know how futile their organization is. How self-defeating. I flip past Frontmen getting chained to a cross by the Forgiveness. Old Americans clashing with the Frontier with knives and pipes in Chicago. I dial through mothers feeding their children wood and dirt. A little boy playing with a dead frog like it was an action figure. Cars stuck in snow, a fistfight taking place outside their windows. People commuting to work, uncaring, unaffected by the chaos outside. I see people bake chicken for dinner. Shopping for clothes, instead of stitching up denim scraps from dumpsters. I look at the old man's body in the corner. *Jesus. You had to watch this all day, every day, for the last 30 years.*

I flip past empty restaurants, sparsely patronized cafes and gas stations packed with lines of cars. Clay would have loved to see all these gas stations. He always had a romantic notion for 'em. Clay... why's he in my mind right now? I saw his face... *no.* I flip back a few feeds and screens to the traffic jam. There's snow on the ground. Montana?

And there he is. Clay. With a teenager who's holding a gun. They're in some kind of altercation with a driver. No, a gang of drivers, now. *No, a gang of Nazis.*

"RUN, YOU IDIOT!" I scream into the screen. I feel embarrassed. I look to the corpse with its flickering shadows. "Like *you* never talked to them."

I look back to the screen. The kid empties his cylinder. Three of the five guys fall dead, pieces of them stark red on the snow. The kid reloads as Clay aims a gun at an approaching Nazi holding a steel baton. Clay shoots and hits the man's shoulder, not enough to knock him down. Nazi brings the baton down Clay's wrist and Clay stumbles onto his ass in the snow. The kid locks his cylinder and shoots. The Nazi falls face first, missing an ear. The fifth man comes up behind the kid and slits his throat. Clay yells and scrambles for his gun.

The dead man's eyes look at me as if I'm supposed to be doing something.

Cold Blooded

Zeph sways with his open throat, too young to recognize that he can be killed. His eyes don't realize it yet as a look of indignant shock freezes into them. He falls on his side. The Nazi wipes his knife on his jacket and turns to Clay.

"Didn't think we'd—" he starts, but four bullets in the stomach cuts him short. He doesn't deserve a speech. He trips over Zeph, falls and dies. And that's all there is to the fight on the snowy road in Montana. Clay hoists himself up and brushes off his pants and jacket. People are staring.

Let 'em stare. He's lost two friends today. Two good Scum. He might even lose a third. But he'd have to find Carly first. At first he thinks that the trail is lost with the capsized truck but then he realizes that without a car—and you couldn't drive a car out of this mess—you'd have to go on foot. And there's no way Carly walked away out of that crash without an injury. Clay hushes the clamoring motorists around him to focus on the blood on the ground, trying to decipher Carly's from the Nazis' and Zeph's. He finds a trail of peach-tinged snow leading into the traffic, *of course, she wouldn't double back*, past a few dozen cars before heading north, along with some boot prints, into the woods.

Clay checks his cylinder. One shot left. He checks his pockets and hears a jangle. He brings out three cartridges and pushes them through the loading gate. He sighs and continues into the dim evergreen maze, holding his broken wrist with his good hand, the gun in the limp one. Maybe he's hoping he'll miss.

Snow-laden branches wet his shoulders as he stumbles and falters through the trees. He keeps an eye to the ground, focusing on distinguishing the impressions made by feet from the irregular terrain of the forest floor. Which means Clay runs his face into the errant branch of blackberry bramble, swearing as he untangles himself, using his pistol to separate thorn from cloth. Oh, my sweet Clay. You lanky, skeletal orangutan. Grace was never your strong suit. Still, he's able to clear his jacket from the mess of bramble and spill into a small clearing where he collects himself, shivering.

Carly's there, lying on her back and smoking a cigarette. A gash bleeds just under her ribs. Carly makes no effort to add pressure to it. She takes a drag and lets the smoke ruin her insides. Her head rests on a shiny, metal box wrapped in black and yellow tape. Carly smiles.

"Bruise! You made it." Carly removes a beer can from her pocket and pops it. "Hope you have a beer ready, I think my ship is just about sunk." She takes a slurp, followed by a drag, followed by a smokey belch.

"Carly!" says Clay. "What are you doing?" He waves the pistol inquisitively.

"Oh," muses Carly. "It looks like you've brought a gun to a bomb fight." Carly cackles and coughs. "Really, though, how boring. Sure, they're fun, with their noises and loud bangs, but what's that compared to my little Christmas present all wrapped up in pretty tape?" Carly hiccups and winces. "It's going to be a White Christmas."

"It's July."

"Oh, well, then Happy Independence Day." Carly shrugs and swigs beer.

"I can't let you launch a nuke. Fun's fun, but this is just evil. You know what'll happen if you hit that button."

"Kablooie. I got it."

"No, another world war. Or something. Something bad."

Carly looks hurt.

"We wasn't going to hit a city. Hell, we hadn't even chosen a target yet. I was thinking this big-ass wall to Canada, close enough that I could see it shine. Doesn't that sound nice? A little ray of sunshine in these dark times? Well, for a second anyway. Kablooie! One big white flash before the big nothing."

"That's why you were heading north through the woods?"

Carly flicks her cigarette away from her and pulls out another one.

"Might not've shot the thing off at all. Who knows? I just wanted to ride the rails of some real adventure for once. You get acclimated to the Scum life. You build a tolerance for it. So does the rest of the world. Starts to feel a little pointless after a while. Wouldn't it be nice to remind everybody that we've still got some fight in us? Remind everyone that we can be just as dangerous as the powers that be?" Carly whistles a tune. Clay can't place it. It sounds somewhat upbeat. She stops suddenly and frowns.

"But I get you, Bruise. People gotta live and they don't like doing it in fear. Well, people who ain't Scum, anyway. Scum ain't got to do anything they don't wanna do." *Slurp.* "And a good Scum loves fear."

Clay thumbs the cylinder of his pistol nervously. He tries to find the moon through the trees. He almost spots the drone that's broadcasting this reunion to my screen.

He asks, "What do you want to do?"

Carly shrugs. She takes a drag and says, "I don't know. I'm getting bored. You want to get out of here?"

Clay's taken aback but he looks relieved. "You and me?"

"You, me, and the threat of annihilation. Sound like a good crew?"

Clay thinks that he's had better friends, but he also can't remember where he left them. *Love the bomb you're with.*

Clay pulls Carly up from the snow.

He asks, "Where are we going to go?"

"How 'bout Scum Haus?" asks Carly.

"Home," confirms Clay.

Carly lifts the nuclear football from the ground and the weight makes her left shoulder sag, forcing blood from her wound. She hands it to Clay.

They walk back to the traffic jam, Carly whistling.

Plague by Law

Reeve looks over his shoulder resting on the back of the booth. There's hardly anyone dining in FORK N PORK'S DINER AND LOUNGE despite it being mid-morning. Xavier's half loaded on a Bloody Mary that just had a whole piece of bacon dropped on top of the ice as garnish. Denilles hasn't said a single word the entire time, possibly because of the knife that Rebecca lets rest on his fly zipper. Coffees and beers sit on the table at varying levels of finished, circling an unused pack of cards, Xavier's.

Reeve clears his throat.

"What now?" He addresses the question to Rebecca.

"Now we wait until Fulter's confirmed dead."

"Didn't we do that already with the heart monitor in Gary's room?" asks Reeve.

Rebecca answers, "We wait until my people confirm

that he's dead."

"So we do nothing," says Reeve. "We sit and what, wait for a phone call?"

"That's the plan," says Rebecca, tight lipped.

"Damn, Becky," says Reeve. "You had this thing all planned out to a T, huh?"

Under the table, Rebecca shifts the knife away from Denilles and tickles Reeve's knee pit with the edge before moving it back to Denilles.

"I told you not to call me that. Ever."

Xavier burps. He says, "What're we doing with the nerd, then?" He blows a kiss at Denilles.

"Insurance," says Rebecca. "If we have to hold another election."

Gary Denilles looks as if he's a bit uncomfortable. He starts his sentence three different times before pressure from the sawtooth side of Rebecca's blade compels him to come out with it.

"He's dead. You saw on the monitor."

Rebecca: "I just want to be careful. Fulter found a way to hack the frequencies to cause a heart attack. He may have found a way to shut off the frequency entirely."

"To fake his own death?" Xavier asks. "Good move."

Denilles says, "Listen, it doesn't matter whether he's dead or not. Are you not paying attention? They don't even need to look for me. They already know that we're here."

Reeve doesn't take his eyes from the door.

Rebecca says, "So what. It's not like they can just

replace you without some sort of explanatory narrative."

"You're not listening," says Denilles, a bubble of panic accompanying his voice. "They're watching us. Right now, they're watching us."

Rebecca flicks her knife, incising Denilles's knee in a clean, straight cut up to his thigh. He chokes back a yelp, with tears, and spasms, trying not to make any further noise.

"This isn't the time for paranoia, *Gary*," she whispers. "Ask yourself: if they come for you, would you rather leave here on two legs or in a body bag?" Rebecca pats the edge side of her knife against his stomach.

A nervous sweat breaks over Gary's forehead. He stifles it with a long pull of his beer until the glass is empty.

"Ask *yourself*," he begs, "why haven't they come yet?"

Gary Denilles rubs his forehead, leaving red trail marks. "Why haven't they come yet?" he repeats. His eyes stare at nothing. Denilles opens his mouth to say something, but chokes it down. He takes a breath and exhales. He assumes composure. He stands up.

"Excuse me," he says before flipping the table. Xavier gets a crotch full of hot coffee. Reeve gets Bloody Mary in his eyes. Rebecca lashes out with the knife, only nicking Gary's elbow as he pounces over the seat of the booth. It's a surprising display of agility for a man in his mid-50s.

"Aw HELL," yells Rebecca, wiping beer and coffee from her arms. To Reeve and Xavier: "Well, it's been a pleasure, gentlemen. Consider yourselves free from your contract to the Just." She sheathes her knife. "If I find you in Salt Lake City, I'm not going to ask you any questions, I'm just going to kill you."

And with that, Rebecca ran outside. Reeve and Xavier hear a car motor start and tires peeling out of the gravel parking lot. A waitress waits for Reeve to get all of the vodka and tomato juice out of his eyes before she pumps the action of a shotgun, intimating the message that the Frontmen are no longer welcome in this establishment. Xavier throws a two-dollar tip into the mess of broken glassware and various liquids. Pretty generous, given the circumstances.

Outside, Xavier guesses the time by the sun's location in the sky. He figures it's something like 9 am. Reeve scans the road for any sign of Rebecca or Denilles. No dice.

Reeve asks, "Probably thumbed the first car he saw. Do you think he'd go north or south?"

Xavier shrugs. "Doesn't matter. Up to the driver, anyway. You think Rebecca'll find him?"

Reeve exhales. "Don't care. What about you? Do you want to go north or south?"

"Where are we?"

"Not exactly sure. The last sign I saw was for Peoria before we stopped."

"We got friends around here?"

"There's a Frontmen office in Des Moines."

"That's not too bad."

Reeve scans the horizon. He sees nothing but road, corn and soybean fields. The buzzing noise in the air, cicadas he figures, sends a quiet chill through his spine.

Xavier says, "Probably best to make it to the nearest city, get out of the sticks for a bit." He bounces on his heels, eager to move. "Should we hoof it, do you think? Or maybe we can steal us a car." He whistles. "I ain't hitchhiking here, that's for sure."

Reeve stares at the farmland around him, studying the cornfields a hundred yards away.

"That sneaky son of a bitch," he says, crossing the road. He looks at the drainage ditch and finds some freshly pressed mud with footprints tracking east, towards the corn stalks.

"Well, I'll be," laughs Xavier. "He must've ran across the road and laid flat until Rebecca charged down the road in a rage."

"I bet that's right," says Reeve. He unholsters his .38 and hops to the other side of the ditch, treading mud and soy seedlings. He turns to Xavier, putting a finger to his mouth, signaling quiet. The cicadas are screaming.

The mud's smeared up to their shins by the time they reach the cornfield.

Reeve whispers, "We should split up."

Xavier whispers, "In a *corn maze*?"

"It's not a corn maze, it's in rows."

"Still."

"Fine."

It's harder to track the prints between the stalks.

Debris from fallen corn husks and weeds litters the ground, over a layer of hay. Still, they creep quietly through the field, eyes alert for any trace of movement. Xavier thinks he hears something and stops. Reeve can't get the cicadas out of his head. He focuses more on visual clues— and finds one. Recently broken leaves on the stalks caused by someone in a hurry to get to the other side. *Did he see us coming?*

Reeve points at his discovery and motions to follow him, walking fifteen paces ahead of the vandalized foliage before sliding through the corn, gun first.

Gary Denilles is waiting for him on the other side, bound with duct tape and revisiting his life's greater mistakes with a look of self-disappointment. Gary rests at the feet of a man in a sheriff's uniform, who bounces a shotgun casually in his hands. He looks like a beaver with a short, gray mustache.

Reeve's taken aback.

Sheriff says, "Drop your firearm, boy, before you piss y'self. The corn's overwatered as is."

Reeve slowly puts his pistol on the ground.

He says, "I didn't know there was any law enforcement in the area."

The man ignores this, instead calling to someone Reeve can't see. "You get the other one?"

A voice answers, "We got 'em, boss."

"Bring 'im here," Sheriff says, nearly yawning. He wipes his eye with a dirty finger.

Xavier stumbles through the leaves, followed by

another man with another shotgun.

The sheriff looks at his deputy. "Weapon?" His deputy nods and tosses Xavier's pistol into the mud. Sheriff looks to Xavier. "That all of you?" Xavier nods.

To Reeve: "He telling the truth?"

"Yes, sir."

Sheriff chuckles. "Callin' me sir, boy? Making me feel like an old man." He scratches a sunburnt ear. "I suppose you boys aren't from around here."

"Idaho," says Xavier. Reeve winces. *Name, rank and serial number, idiot.*

"Idaho," repeats Sheriff. "You all grow potatoes over in Idaho, as I understand."

"Yep," says Xavier.

"Well, that explains a whole lot, doesn't it, Brody?"

The deputy says, "Not sure I follow, Sheriff."

"Well, when we heard on the radio that there was some riffraff rooting through ole Smithy's cornfield, we didn't expect to find any local boys, now did we?"

"I wasn't expecting no local boys, Sheriff," says Deputy Brody with a broad smile.

"And that's because there ain't no one from around here that doesn't know that ole Smithy likes to solve his trespassin' troubles with a wheat thresher. Keeps most folk out and away." Sheriff pauses to wipe his mustache. "But Idaho?" He barks a laugh. "Well, hell, I bet you potato-eatin' hillbillies didn't even know what a cornstalk looked like before today."

Reeve says nothing, staring at the ground, joining

Denilles in the practice of self-disappointment. *For the love of God, Xavier, keep your mouth shut.*

Sheriff bends down to retrieve Reeve's pistol, exposing a blistering red bald patch. When he rises again, he asks Reeve, still refusing to make eye contact, "You know what a corn stalk looks like?"

"Can't say I've ever seen one before today," says Reeve.

"That's right. You're dumb as rocks. Remember that."

Sheriff walks belly out over to Xavier, bends down and retrieves the pistol from the mud.

"How about you, son? You ever seen an ear of corn in your life?"

Xavier says, "Of course I have."

Sheriff *tut-tuts* in exaggerated disapproval.

"Son, you're telling me that you knew better and you went ahead and trespassed anyway. Brody, what do we call that?"

"We call that a shame, boss."

"We do, indeed. Such a smart boy, too. It's a shame."

Sheriff pockets a pistol, trains the other one on Xavier, and lazily aims the double barrel at Reeve.

"Should've been a dumb rock like your buddy here," he says. "Tie 'em up, would ya Brody?"

"Absolutely, boss."

Brody leans his shotgun against a cornstalk carefully and then produces a roll of duct tape, walking towards Reeve first.

"Okie dokie, boys. Let's get them stomachs dirty. Come on now."

Reeve looks at the mud and straw and back at Brody.

"You kidding me?"

"Alright, well maybe let's make it easier for me then."

Brody places a sharp kick to Reeve's chin, laying him out cold. Brody turns him over and binds his arms behind his back, tapes his ankles together. Finished, he wipes his hands on his jeans and looks to Xavier.

"If there was a time for you to be smart, I reckon it'd be about now."

Xavier lies flat on his stomach, face to the mud. Brody gets him hog-tied and Sheriff calls for the truck.

When Reeve comes to, the first thing he realizes is that he's moving. Life is bumpy and vibrating. When his vision clears he can see that he's in the bed of a pickup truck, next to Xavier, who's had his mouth taped over, and across from a worried Denilles... and a smug looking Brody.

"Rise and shine, buttercup," Brody says. "You boys in it now. But don't you worry, we're getting you to where you need to go. You know where that is? Do you know what you need to do, now?"

Reeve doesn't say anything. Xavier mumbles through his tape. Reeve tries to kick him to shut up.

"You boys gotta repent. Sinners, the both of you. This one too," Brody says, jerking a thumb at Denilles. "He looks guilty as the Devil himself, don't he?" Brody spits, thankfully out towards the road. "And we got to get you to the repentin' place."

The truck slows on the highway. Reeve sees something in a ditch. Then another. And another. He doesn't admit to what they are until the fifth. The somethings: hands, calves, feet, ears, scalps...

Xavier notices something in the sky. He nudges Reeve to acknowledge it. It appears to be floating at first glance, but when the sun clears from their vision, they recognize a familiar image: it's a torso crucified on a phone pole by its arms. Nothing below the navel.

"Welcome to the repentin' place," says Brody, smiling. "We're gonna get that sin out of you."

The car pulls to the side of the road where a gathering of people stand waiting, all wearing red robes.

"Father," Reeve hears Sheriff call out from the window. "We got you some more converts."

Tight Wire

My body reels from panic and chooses a dull sense of boredom as counterweight. It's a coping mechanism. My body and mind are exhausted. I'm short of breath as I scroll back through the feeds, trying to take my mind off things. Those Frontmen are boned. Clay and that Carly girl are still treading snow in between cars in that traffic jam. Who'd have thought that people holding the launch button for a nuclear bomb could be so damn *boring*?

I am not bored. I am panicked and I am coping.

I need to do something. Do I need to do something *fast*? My assumption is yes. Evidence? No. Wait. Maybe. There's a quick little red blip in the corner of the room, just behind me. I catch a glimpse of it when spinning in my new chair. It's faint. I stop spinning and stand on the chair to inspect it. A little glass circle. A camera flush with the wall? Possibly. Actually, what else could it be? A red light blips behind the black glass, ever so softly. I rub off some of the dead woman's makeup from my lip and smear it over the lens.

What have they seen so far?

It doesn't matter. What matters is that I have a deadline. Work the adrenaline back up, Riley. I get up to lock the door. There's no lock. On this side. I drag Mr. O'Brien and prop him up against it. Okay. What tools do I have? I have the same tools that O'Brien had, except that I have no knowledge as to what those are. Except this: O'Brien kept an eye on the Inner Circle so that he could inform the powers that be of any real threat to the state. Which means that there's a communication device in this room.

In fact, I know there is. When Denny and I were lost in the desert on the other side of the wall, we were rescued. Which means that there was a communication device in this room. He had to have ordered a rescue chopper for us. Right? Or could he have told one of the Servicemen to call in to the chopper. But no, the location was specific, in the middle of nowhere. O'Brien needed the coordinates and to be able to update those coordinates for the helicopter pilot. I think. It's a good bet, at least.

Roll through some screens. Flip the toggles. Onscreen, I see a bird's eye view of a rigidly designed city with pure chaos spilling out into the streets. Crews of yellow jumpsuits with black hats and balaclavas ride around in jeeps, collecting their own and mobilizing. A few toggles.

A small screen adjacent to the main console— the one that displays names, ages, blood types and lottery numbers of the faces it recognizes— switches to the geographical coordinates: 40.7608° N, 111.8910° W.

"HA!"

Okay, wheel back to Montana, the snowy road, the snowy road… got it.

Now: comm device, comm device. Look for a microphone. A radio? There isn't one. Maybe it's another form of communication. Morse code? Goddamned semaphore? Come on machine, give me something. I slap the console, if only to make myself feel better.

Check the eye in the wall. Is the lipstick enough to blur the camera? Think about that for a second. Think about Clyde O'Brien, a sad old man who thought of himself as the Devil watching over his dominion when he himself was being monitored.

"I haven't read as much as you, old man," I say to the corpse. "But even I know there are many demons in hell."

He said so himself that he had 'help.'

Sit back in the dead man's chair. Your chair. For the time being. Okay, Riley, get it together. *Breathe.* I know that I can call in an extraction of Clay and Carly. Maybe even deliver them a message. But would they do it on a crowded road? No. But there's a drone camera zipping around the woods, and maybe I can pull the coordinates and land a chopper there. Flip to the forest clearing, visible footprints left by Clay and Carly. Coordinates. Memorize them. Say them aloud three times.

Clay and Carly should be easy to find on the road from here. Carly's wounded, so they'd be moving slowly. What next. *Think.*

A rattle comes from the floor above. The front door opening? There's weight shifting around on the floorboards. A lot of weight. Servicemen. They're going to clear the first floor and see the carnage in the kitchen. Then they're going to clear the upstairs. No, first they'd split up, send a team upstairs and a team downstairs.

Think.

I have a bomb. I just don't know what to point it at. What coordinates do I have? I scroll through some screens. Fields. Buildings. Stores. Homes. Nothing. I look at the eye in the wall with its rouge smear. A theory: If Clyde O'Brien was being monitored then he had to have someone monitoring him. The other Presidents. The other demons. His 'help.'

Flip the toggle, roll the wheel, find the right feed. Interior cameras. Now we're getting somewhere. People eating dinner. A man on the toilet. Children playing with toy guns. Another toggle, more random images of little lives. More useless— wait. The shoulders and head of a man at a console like this one. Flip the toggle. 47.6062° N, 122.3321° W. Say it aloud three times. Say the Montana code three times. Say this one again, three times. I got you now, you bastards.

I've got the what and the where. I just need the how. Come on, Riley, *think.*

Footsteps on the stairs. *Think.* O'Brien wanted you to

do something. He planned for this to happen. He gave you something. He gave you a bomb. Did he tell you how to use it? There's no ink or paper here. Just a guitar. Look on the back. Nothing. On the neck? Nothing. Smash the guitar on the ground. Nothing written on the inside. *He would have had to have left a message in such a way that the camera behind him couldn't see.* I look at the smiling corpse against the door. *Aw, man. It's on his goddamn body, isn't it?*

The door knob turns and tries to open. Clyde's body holds it shut. For now. Run to the corpse. Check under his sleeves, behind his neck. Bangs against the door now. It opens just a crack. *Somewhere the camera couldn't see.* Check his stomach. Think about unzipping his pants, but would rather die. Three gloved fingers pop out of the door. Jump up to slam it shut. The fingers disappear, but Clyde falls on his side. Roll up the cuffs of his pants. And there it is, scratched into the skin around his ankle with, probably, a piece of guitar wire:

EXFIL: 3 SWITCH UNDRNTH

Boots bashing against the door now. Clyde giving way. Not sure what "exfil" means. Run to the console. Three switches underneath. Underneath what? The desk? Oh. Sure enough, three blue switches. Check the door. An arm's loose through the door. Flip the switches one by one, hope to Christ there's no specific order. I went from left to right. Get up off my hands and jump into a swan kick against the door, hopefully shattering the arm's elbow. The arm retreats. Curses. Reposition Clyde as best as I can. Back to the console.

The screen has changed.

It's now completely blue with a query at the top and a key pad below to type an answer. The query:

EXTRACTION POINT:

I type against the screen. The coordinates for the clearing in the Montanan woods and hope to Christ I got it right. Another prompt:

TARGET(S):

I type, "TALL LANKY MALE, MEDIUM BUILD, INJURED FEMALE. CARRYING BRIEFCASE. WALKING."

MESSAGE:

"CLAY. RILEY. LAUNCH IT. 47.6062° N, 122.3321° W. TRUST ME."

O.R. AIRPORT FACILITIES NEARBY. EST. EXTRACTION TIME 15 MINUTES.

The door clangs open, a foot wide. I sit in the chair—*my* chair—and face away. I hear Clyde's body shoved aside and the boots of what I estimate to be six to eight soldiers file in. I hear the metallic symphony of automatic riles preparing for fire. I'm calm. The hand I'm about to play contains a nuclear bomb potentially falling on Seattle. That should ensure a reaction from the Outer Ring, which should ensure a reaction from other nations. A royal flush. Enough to get me out. I spin around, leisurely.

"Gentlemen, so nice of you to join me," I say with as coy a smile as I can muster. I flex my fingers. "Here's the situation. I've ordered a nuclear bomb to be dropped somewhere on the west coast. If you cooperate with me, we can call it off and get—"

A soldier says, "Light her up."

The muzzle flashes are blinding as each gun releases a three bullet burst. The console whizzes and sparks and screens around me shatter and explode in a spectacle of miniature fireworks. The bullets rip up my chest and I slump into my seat.

The chair spins softly in a room of spent gunpowder.

Hail Rat King

It comes down from the sky, like a mechanical bird with lights, hovering over their heads, blasting snow into the cars and into curious travelers' faces. Then it descends and disappears into the woods.

Carly says, "Let's check it out."

Clay's unsure, but figures that any kind of transportation that could get Carly to a hospital quicker was worth gambling on. They retrace their steps, shoving gawkers and rubberneckers alike out of the way, hunching to reenter the woods, following Carly's blood trail back to the clearing.

The helicopter's waiting, motor off, blades softly turning.

Three uniformed soldiers jump out and raise rifles. Clay raises his hands, his pistol safely tucked in the back of his jeans. Carly smiles, clutching her side, the silver briefcase in the other. A soldier looks them over.

"Are you Clay?" he asks gruffly.

Clay nods. The soldier makes a lowering gesture with his hands and the rifles are pointed to the ground. The soldier approaches and extends a piece of paper. Clay accepts it, sweating in the cold, and unfolds it to read.

"Riley," he says out loud.

"Riley?" asks Carly. "Who's Riley?"

"My…" begins Clay. "…ex-girlfriend." He passes the note to Carly, whose expression moves from confused to downright giddy.

"I like her," she says, dropping the briefcase on the ground and opening it.

"You sure about this?" asks Clay, nervously, eyeing the rifles.

"Your girlfriend sure seems to be," says Carly.

The soldier asks, "What is that?" before musing, "Is that…" before silently answering his question. His gun is back up, trained on Carly.

"Approach cautiously," says the soldier. "This is not a drill. They have the bomb."

And the other guns are up.

"Clay," says Carly, waving dismissively at the soldiers. "Would you, please?"

Clay gulps.

"Move away from the briefcase, lady," says the point man.

"We'll give you to the count of three," says a grunt behind him.

"One."

Clay shuts his eyes. He can hear Carly keying in the coordinates. *This is really happening.*

"Two."

Channel Zeph, Clay. Be like the Zen scum rat prince the boy once was. Honor his death.

"Thr—"

Clay pulls the pistol out of his jeans and fires three shots, slapping the hammer down with his tree hand each time. All six eyes behind the balaclavas freeze with a look of shock before lifting to the sky. The three bodies hit the snow softly.

"Damn, Bruise. Never knew you had it in you," says Carly. She smiles at him. That makes Clay happy inside.

"You forgot something," she says, nodding behind him.

The pilot. Clay turns to fire, his broken wrist seizing, throwing the bullet harmlessly into the woods. The pilot puts a bullet over Clay's shoulder. So close Clay can feel the heat on his ear. Clay attempts to fire again to the tune of an empty chamber. The pilot's turn. He sends bark flying from a tree next to Clay. Pilot again. Clay stops. His gun arm goes numb and he drops the pistol into red snow.

"Christ's sake," says Carly. Clay can barely see her move as she jumps up from the briefcase, runs serpentine to the pilot and presses her palm against his esophagus, driving him against the helicopter. Clay hears a wet crunch.

"Whew," says Carly, bouncing back to her feet. She

wanders back to the case. The coordinates are in. She turns a key. She looks at Clay.

"Are we sure about this?" she asks, in a surprisingly gentle, scared voice.

Clay sighs. "My ex-girlfriend sure seems to be."

"It's just…" Carly says, "…I always wanted to do it. Just to see it. But don't think I don't know what turning this key means."

"I'm won't doubt you there," says Clay, rubbing his bullet wound. "But I don't want to doubt Riley either. If she's in a position to give us this message, it's probably the right message."

"Okay," exhales Carly. She turns the other key. The blue button in the center begins to flash. The two share another look. Silently, they press the button together.

The button stops flashing and the digital display of the keyed in coordinates shuts off. They stand and watch the thing.

"How do we know that it worked?" asks Clay.

"I think we'll know soon enough," says Carly.

She takes Clay's numb hand and squeezes it. Clay wishes he could have actually felt it but appreciates the gesture. They watch the cloud white sky above as snow collects on their faces.

"It's not our problem anymore," says Carly. "You want to get out of here?"

Clay shakes snow out of his hair. "You know how to drive that thing?"

"No," she says. "But it's all the same, ain't it? Like

riding a bicycle."

Carly squeezes Clay's hand again and they walk over to the helicopter, climbing into the cockpit and strapping themselves in. Carly lifts the throttle and the rotors begin spinning. She increases the throttle until the chopper is off the ground. The tips of conifer branches fly in every direction as the rotors trim nearly every tree upon their ascent It's a rough ride, but the blades don't seem to have incurred much damage. Clay hears a crunching noise as he clutches his seatbelt. He sees bits of plastic and wiring scatter to the wind— the remains of a camera drone.

Soon they're above the trees. The chopper wavers in the wind, but otherwise seems steady.

"Nothing to it," says Carly, producing two canned beers from her jacket pocket. She hands one to Clay, pops hers open and takes a deep pull. "Where to?"

They hear thunder off in the distance and the snow white clouds take on a neon quality.

"We could go to Canada," says Clay. "Fly over the wall, get out of the States. Seems like a good time to go."

"They have beer there, I think," says Carly.

"Whiskey, too," says Clay.

"Yeah, maybe," says Carly. She works the pedals to point the chopper north.

Another thunder crash. The clouds have a slight pink tinge to them. Carly rests her hands on the control stick.

Clay's stomach turns, unsure if he wants to say what he's going to say.

"Or…" he begins. "It's kind of rude to cut and run, if you know what I mean."

"I think I do," says Carly, grinning.

Clay pops his beer open. He says, "Let's go back to Scum Haus."

Carly raises her beer. "One for all, and we're all fucked."

"Hail Rat King," says Clay.

They cheers and drink together. Carly points the chopper west and noses it forward, chasing an odd and beautiful neon light.

Non-Penitent Thieves

Sheriff and Deputy Brody drag Reeve, Xavier and Gary Denilles out onto the gravel, putting them on their knees in a line. The small crowd of red-robed figures regard them with disgust. A man with a uniquely ornate robe lined with gold thread comes forward and inspects the faces of the prisoners brought before him.

"Sinners," he says definitively. "I can see it your eyes. But I can see deeper than the layer of filth that has accumulated on your soul. I can see that you men seek redemption. I can hear your souls begging for it." He paces back and forth during this sermon. "I am here to tell you that redemption is on its way. With the righteous hand of our good Lord, you shall be cleansed." He nods to Sheriff and Brody, who are leaning against their truck, watching approvingly. "You are upstanding fishers of men, Truth Bearers. I suppose you'd like to stay and watch the Lord's work?"

Sheriff smiles. "It does my soul good to witness faith in action, Father."

Father smiles back. "It does indeed. And you, my son?" He asks Brody.

"Same for me, Father," Brody says, putting a dip of chewing tobacco in his lip.

"Very well." Father turns to his flock. "Before we begin the ceremony, I am delighted to announce that we have a celebrity convert in our midst." Father heel turns to Denilles. "Gary Denilles. The infamous mathematician, inventor of the Voting Machine. You are a smart man, Mr. Denilles. But did you use your intelligence in the service of our Lord?"

Gary Denilles stumbles through his answer. "I… I… I served m-my c-country in the best way that I c-could."

Father says, "Putting country before God is honorable only to cynics and atheists!" The robed congregation spit and hiss.

Denilles protests, attempting to appeal to the zealotry threatening him. "Th-this is a Christian nation, F-father. It's one and the s-same, isn't it?"

Father chuckles. "My son. You are quite correct." He puts a hand on Denilles's shoulder. "This *is* a Christian nation." He removes the hand. "But it has fallen into disrepair and you, Mr. Denilles, are an agent of that disrepair. You cherish your mind, but the mind is a hindrance to the soul's truest desire to be with God. The mind is a slave to the body, in turn a slave to Satan.

Repent now and be welcomed into the loving embrace of the Holy Father."

"I-I repent," stumbles Denilles.

"That's good, child," says Father soberly. "You have saved yourself from an eternal life of insufferable hellfire." He extends his hands. An acolyte places a communion wafer in one hand, a machete in the other. Father places the communion wafer on Denilles's tongue. Gary chews and chokes down the dry cracker.

"Sheriff, if you would," says Father.

Sheriff steps forward and cuts the duct tape binding Denilles's hands before stepping back to his truck. Father turns to his robed followers. "This man put his hands to work against the Lord's design. I quote from Mathew: If your right hand makes you stumble…" Father grabs Gary by the arm and raises the machete. "…Cut it off and throw it from you." Father takes off Gary Denilles's right hand. An acolyte steps forward and accepts it. Denilles falls into a state of shock, too dumbfounded to even scream in pain. "Accept this sacrifice, Lord, and be happy with your children who ask for your forgiveness, and let your fury fall on those who refuse it."

Denilles's face is ghost-white and his vocal cords are warming up as his senses begin to return. Reeve turns his face away and shuts his eyes while Xavier looks on with mortified curiosity. Brody snickers and Sheriff hits him gently to shut up, concealing a smile himself.

Father's sermon continues.

"This poor man engineered a machine that perverted

this land of grace, going against the gears of the Holy Father's design. Fear not, child! For the wretched hubris of man's wisdom will be outed as Satan's folly in the illumination of God's will!"

Denilles croaks syllables in response.

Father: "I quote Corinthians, the First: I will destroy the wisdom of the wise; the intelligence of the intelligent I will frustrate." Father raises the machete with both hands.

Denilles stutters, "T-t-dt-dt-t—"

Father yells, "NOW FLEE, CHILD!" and brings the blade downward with a crack. After it's over, Reeve opens his eyes to see Father holding Gary Denilles's head to the crowd. He hears Brody spit behind him.

"Another soul saved! He is free! Free of Satan! Free of sin!" he calls to the congregation, who cheer and holler. When they calm, Father awkwardly passes the head to an acolyte, muttering "Here, do something with this."

Father turns to Reeve and Xavier, winding his charismatic fervor back down to a gentle whisper, wiping the machete clean with his robe.

"Now, you sinners. Do you repent the sins of the body and wish to join your Father in Heaven?"

Reeve and Xavier answer in unison, "NO."

Father says, "Just as the non-penitent thief, you two shall not be with Him in paradise today," before adding more gravely, "but you will hang justly for your deeds."

"It's okay, Xavier," Reeve whispers to Xavier. "It'll be okay."

There are tears in Xavier's eyes. "No, man. Not really. But thanks anyway."

Red robed acolytes come forward with ropes and pocket knives. The tape is cut and replaced with rope, around the hands and feet and looped twice around the waist. Brody hunches down and whispers in Reeve's ear.

"You know what's gonna to happen, right? They're gonna hoist you up and let you bake in the sun for three days. On the third day, if you're lucky, they're gonna come back and chop your heads off. Should've repented, boys. But then again, I suppose you're too smart for that, right?" He slaps Reeve on the back of his head.

Pulley ropes are slung over the telephone wires and tied to the knot around their waists. While the crucifixion is being prepared, Xavier notices that someone has set up a table with two carafes of coffee and a plate of cookies and brownies. The hoods are lowered and Father laughs and converses with Sheriff while other members speak freely about work and children and gardening.

Reeve overhears Father say, "You mean that little Allie baked these? Incredible. No, better keep them away from me, I'll eat the whole dang tray!" Reeve's head spins, partially out of incredible rage and confusion, partially because of the disorienting effect of his feet leaving solid ground as he's yanked into the air by the pulley. The congregation below doesn't even bother to watch. Reeve's whole body floats on anxious vertigo. When he reaches the top, the robed acolytes below tie off the rope to a climbing peg below. Brody climbs up the pole himself to momentarily untie the hand and feet restraints, only to rebind them again to the crossarm.

"Careful, now," Brody says. "Wouldn't want you to fall."

Reeve fantasizes about kicking Deputy Brody in the stomach, sending him earthbound. He fights the urge, knowing that vengeance would come to Xavier first and then himself. The stench of chewing tobacco on Brody's whistling lips is wretched. Reeve grimaces through it, like he does everything else. When Brody's work is done, Reeve's wrists are each tied to the wooden cross bar, his legs singularly bound to the pole and his stomach snugly fit with rope so to, as Brody explains, "Keep you from suffocating into a coward's death." Before Brody descends he slaps Reeve's face gently.

"There you go. All tucked in."

The process repeats for Xavier who joins Reeve in a matter of minutes. Once his ropes are tied and Brody again descends with a bastardly comment, the congregation below organizes once again.

"What are they doing?" Xavier asks.

"I think," Reeve says, craning and, subsequently, straining his neck, "they're singing."

A hymn carries up from below, although neither of the Frontmen can place the tune. At first. Then Reeve gets it. He lets a single, sardonic laugh escape from his nose.

"They're singing the goddamn national anthem."

"Heh," says Xavier, but clearly doesn't find it amusing.

From up there, they can see for miles. Xavier takes a moment to take in the new sight, acclimating himself to the vantage. Corn and soy for miles, atop rolling hills spotted with barns, tiny towns wedged between valleys. It all looks so harmless from above. The roads snake through everything, black rivers of pavement, stitching together an imperfect quilt. In the distance, on one of those roads, Xavier sees something. A black dot, glinting in the sun.

"Reeve," Xavier says. "Do you see that?"

"See what?"

"That!"

The black dot gains speed then slows around the corners of the road. Soon Reeve can see it too out of the corner of his eye. It's a motorcycle, just like the one he owned once. An earthly treasure. The chorus below swells, unaware of the object closing in. Closer now, the motorcycle slows, maintaining a steady, cautious speed. The congregation of the Forgiveness pay it no mind, except to sing louder to match the hum of the motor. The cyclist bears down on the robed crowd below, taking the bike into the gravel, easing into a slide before jumping and rolling off into the street.

Chaos below as the bike clips four robed figures. The cyclist rallies onto her feet as she darts along the parked cars, unclipping small objects from her vest and depositing them into each open window. Rounding about, she opens fire on the remaining robes gathered across the drainage ditch. Then she dives into the ditch covering her head.

"It's Rebecca! She came for us!" exclaims Xavier. "I knew she would."

"No, you didn't," sighs Reeve.

The shape recognizable as Brody runs to Sheriff's truck to grab his shotguns just in time to catch the brunt of the explosion. One by one, the other cars follow its incendiary suit. Rebecca lets the remaining congregation run down the highway, leveling her pistol at the shape recognizable as Father. His robes have caught fire and Reeve and Xavier can hear him scream clearly. Rebecca decides not to shoot, leaving Father to immolate alone in a field, spreading fire to everything he touches.

The shape recognizable as Sheriff stands and draws Xavier's pistol, that trusty .38. Rebecca turns to face him.

Reeve can't be sure of what he hears over the now roaring fire of the automobile blaze, but he thinks he hears Sheriff say, "Becky?" before lowering his gun. Rebecca puts two shots in his stomach and he stumbles and falls onto his face.

The Rebecca shape is heaving, panting heavily. She looks around for any hidden attackers, finds none and holsters her weapon. She looks up at Xavier and Reeve, pitifully strung up on the telephone pole.

"Denilles with you?" she calls up.

"He's down there!" Xavier calls down. "The headless guy!"

"Can you get us down from here?" calls Reeve.

Rebecca either doesn't hear him or doesn't care. She

looks at Denilles. Then she looks at Sheriff. Then off to nothing. She brushes her knees off and goes to her bike, untangling the wheels from robe and bone, rights it and kicks it to start. The sound of the wheels grating against the gravel is equivalent to the sound of Xavier's heart breaking, along with Reeve's hopes to make it out alive. They watch as the motorcycle weaves back into the river of pavement, through the hills and finally disappearing beyond the horizon.

"She'll be back, right?" asks Xavier.

"Maybe," says Reeve, biting his lip. "Somebody is sure to find us."

"Maybe," Xavier repeats back to him, sounding defeated.

Reeve hears Xavier begin to cry. "Hey, buddy," he says in a weird growl, unaccustomed to comforting his fellow man. "Hey buddy, we might be in the worst possible situation I can think of, but, uh, you know," he coughs, "I'm glad that we're in it together. You know?"

"I know, man. Thanks."

"It sure is pretty up here, ain't it, Xavier?"

"So long as you don't look down."

"Yeah," says Reeve. "Don't look down. We'll just look at that sky and in a weird way, we'll consider ourselves lucky."

"Yeah," says Xavier. "We're going to die, sure as rain. But yeah. This ain't such a bad way to go, all things considered."

"Yeah, we could have repented."

Xavier laughs. "Yeah, we still got a head on our shoulders."

"It ain't nothing."

A gentle wind whips at their faces as they look around, kings of a strange and warped kingdom. The gas tanks of the cars ignite one by one. The fire from the cars meets the grass fire from Father's immolation. Reeve and Xavier catch a good deal of smoke.

"Man, Rebecca sure got them good."

"I knew she would."

The blue sky invites a sudden azure tinge to its palette. Xavier remarks on its beauty. Reeve agrees.

They pass the time as two friends, each immobile, suspended one hundred and twenty feet in the air, crucified amidst a world of madness, death, and beauty.

Some Bright Morning

The soldiers don't waste much time confirming their kill, they just take a cursory look at my limp body and take me for a goner. No mercy shot. The point man radios everything in.

I hear, "Yeah, we got her. O'Brien's dead. Barnes has a few broken fingers and Farley has a shattered elbow. We'll order a cleanup crew for the house after we get them checked into med. It's a bloodbath upstairs. Haven't seen anything like it. Yeah. Roger that. Over and out."

The point man makes a sharp gesture with his hands and everyone files out. He snakes Clyde's bottle of Tennessee sour mash, gives the room another once-over and nods, satisfied. He leaves with the receding sound of congratulatory statements of his team.

They leave me to my thoughts, spinning nearly dead in my chair. Breathing's shallow to nonexistent, oxygen failing to refresh my brain. My heart seems intent on pumping my blood out of my body, anyway. May as well get it all over the floor. Good a place as any. I won't be using it.

If there's a world tomorrow, I'm going down in history as a monster. They'll say I murdered Denny and Clyde and the Servicemen upstairs. Half right. And then they'd say that I wrought nuclear holocaust upon every living thing on earth. Will they? The soldiers were clueless of my ruse. Ha. Only a ruse. Heavy gamble. The bomb'll drop and then the Outer Ring will launch a payload to whatever country they deem responsible. And then we'll get ours. Anyway, what are the chances that papers will be running? And what's worse? Being remembered as the final plague of mankind, or not being remembered at all? Turns out Clay remembered me. I hope he's happy, I really do. I hope he doesn't mind living in the mess I've made.

I can't be too hard on myself. We're all culpable. All of us gullible. I was given a hand and I played it. Not my fault those guys didn't want to play. Did Clyde know this would happen, too? Maybe not. For my part, my fellow Americans, I'm sorry.

The console is on the fritz, flipping from one screen to another, images splashing over themselves. Overhead: a crushing sound not unlike thunder, followed by an earthquake that shakes the whole house. Here it comes. The retaliation. So stupid. The screens show me peaceful farms, hospitals and quiet city streets. Another earthquake, another crushing noise.

So many people. Should I feel guilty, when I'm one of them? They told us the coasts were nuked into oblivion. So the lie became truth. You gotta be careful with your lies. Heh. The country that cried *bomb*. The room begins to warm. A nuclear inferno awaits outside. The Outer Ring of Hell. So sometimes metaphors come true, too. Gotta be careful with your metaphors.

And I became the Devil. Clyde's smiling at me, slumped over on the floor. Looks pretty pleased with himself. Well, you got your wish, Clyde. You got to die as yourself, pushing the buck to me. I'll take it. Nowhere to spend it now, though. Ha ha. The buck stops here. Kind of neat to think that I'm the last President of the New States. I wonder if they have a VIP room in hell?

One by one the screens on the walls turn dark. The console reports dead images, mixed with still live feeds until nothing appears in its rotation. Another quake shakes the room, but I've got no mind to worry about that now.

My vision's fading. Clyde's smiling over by the door. The last thing I'll see.

I turn to dreams, images bubbling into my mind. Pleasant images accompanied by a gentle, hopeful voice. My own, once upon a time. It tells me that if the world can get through this nightmare, if the country can get push through the horrors it wrought upon itself, then there can start something anew.

The voice tells me that next time, people might be a

little less hostile, the world a little more livable. There might be a happier, freer union. A safer union. One where malevolent organizations don't burn your house down. Where a little girl can walk her dog down the street without having to fear that it might be conscripted and starved to become an attack hound for some political movement for blah-blah-blah… A place where life is worth a decent goddamn.

I hear the voice speak of tomorrow as something to look forward to.

And I can't help but die with a smile.

43611557R00145

Made in the USA
Middletown, DE
14 May 2017